The
Source

The Source

IFUNANYA C. OGOCHUKWU N.

For my family

Part 1

Together

CHAPTER I

The girl with no memories strolled through the forest.

She wandered for what felt like an eternity, unfeeling of the severity of her situation.

Roaming around in a daze, she gazed at her surroundings with bright eyes, taking in the sights with an enthralled stare.

Why didn't she feel the way she thought she would?

Why wasn't she scared or panicked? Confused?

The only thing she picked up on was excitement, deep seated in her very core.

A rush of wonder, watching sunlight filter through the leaves.

A feeling of peace, in a world full of life, devoid of people.

She walked on, no end goal or destination in mind.

Walking for the love of it.

Gazing up at the spindly trees towering over her, she marvelled at their height and the timeless stature they seemed to hold, the swaying branches instilling authority over the plant life. A cool breeze blew over her, seeming to take with it all her worries.

She looked up through the overhead canopy of leaves. A hue of violet tinged the cloudless sky, something that appealed to her in a peculiar way.

She asked herself the question again.

Why wasn't she worried?

Maybe it was because she didn't *want* to get her memories back.

Maybe she liked it better this way.

She considered this prospect, a frown plaguing her features.

Since the time she first woke up here until now, nothing about this bothered her one bit.

Continuing onwards, she approached a wide clearing, brightened by the lack of leaves sheltering it from the sun. She made her way towards it, taking in the distinct smell of earth and leaves and life.

The girl walked to the bark of one especially tall tree.

Her leg found a foot hold, her hand gripped a branch and she hauled herself upwards.

No certain reason called her to climb, but a rush of air against her face and the tickling of leaves on her cheek urged her on. A burst of euphoric adrenaline energised her, and next thing she knew, she was standing among the leafy branches at the top of the tree.

The girl's eyes flew open as she took in the view.

Just past the greenery, she could make out a large body of tranquil turquoise, glittering with reflected sun beams.

The sea.

She was on an island.

A wide grin split the girl's face, any previous worries she had melting away.

What she had been before didn't matter. Maybe it was even better that she had forgotten.

This was now.

And she had a wide world to explore.

The girl stood in awe a while longer, gaping at the picturesque scene before her. Finally, she'd decided that she'd seen enough, and headed back down.

Her smile only grew as she lowered herself to the ground. When was the last time she'd had this much fun?

She tried to remember.

Big mistake.

A stab of agony exploded through her skull. She yelled in pain, squeezing her eyes shut, taking in sharp, agonized breaths. Eventually it subsided, leaving her shaking with fear, clutching her head.

At that moment, she realized something fundamentally crucial.

There was something wrong with this, all of this.

Something very, very wrong.

Trembling and spluttering, she got up. She realised now.

She was alone.

She was alone and defenceless in a place she didn't know.

She didn't know what to do.

What should she do?

She did the only thing she could think of. The only thing that felt familiar.

Laying down on the grass, she shut her eyes.

Shut out the world. Trying not to think.

Trying not to remember.

The girl felt something bud inside her. A surge of energy, faint and tingly until it began to swell, pressure building up steadily in her chest. It grew and grew until she felt as though she was about to burst.

So she let it out.

She rose to her feet, ignoring the dimming ache of her head.

Her hands curled into fists.

She didn't want to ever cower in fear. Over here, in her world, there was nothing to fear. No threats or danger.

No people.

Instead, she vowed to stand tall, no matter what the cost.

Ignoring the slight twitch in her limbs, she continued on her way.

The wonder and magic from just moments ago was gone, and an air of uncertainty plagued her mind.

Doubts mounted in her head.

Where was she going? What was going to happen from here? She tried pushing these thoughts aside. Thinking too much about them wasn't going to make anything easier.

Without warning, the girl stopped, her blue eyes darting around cautiously.

Something wasn't right.

A strange anticipating silence kept her frozen in place, leaving her to listen to the unusual quiet which had overcome the area.

The howl came shortly afterwards, too loud to not be a threat.

It reverberated in the girl's ears, and she knew that she had been right.

Not that that was a good thing.

Panic flooded her system as she sprinted in the opposite direction. Her heart raced wildly, blood pumping in her ears, but she pressed onward, racing through the trees.

That's when she saw it.

A lightning fast streak of grey flashed in the corner of her eye, only just about distinguishable as some sort of animal. She let out a gasp of horror and ran like she never had before.

There was no hope left for her. She was getting tired and slower, the animal was getting nearer. Soon there would be no space between them.

This didn't keep her from moving forward.

She kept going,

and going,

and going.

Leaves crunched under her feet, branches constantly attacked her, and her breaths became ragged as she held in her scream.

Her foot collided with a tree root on the ground.

As if on cue, she stumbled and fell. She crashed into the ground, her face colliding into the dirt. Shielding her face with her arm on instinct, her heart threatened to burst out of her chest, waiting for the impact.

It never came.

She looked up and her eyes widened.

A boy gazed down at her.

He was small and slight, ruffled blonde hair appearing white in the sun. Fern coloured eyes peered down at her, taking in her image, wide and fearful. His expression looked like it was holding all the fear and confusion it could muster.

Their eyes met.

Something clicked in the girl's mind, something so powerful and unprecedented, she couldn't even begin to imagine how she had forgotten.

But now she remembered.

Remembered that this boy was her everything.

That she would kill for him.

And in that moment, he was all that mattered.

The animal slowed down, and eventually, the grey streak became a silvery outline of fur just meters away from them.

A wolf.

The boy's expression was one of fear and confusion as the animal stood from a distance.

"What…is that a wolf?" he whispered, his small voice shaky and fearful.

The girl got up slowly and purposefully, going to the boy's front in a protective manner.

She may not have known anything about her life, but she knew that it wouldn't be worth living anymore if something happened to him.

She could practically feel the boy's stare burning her back.

"Don't attack."

These words caught her so off guard that she turned around to give him a look.

His eyes held fear, caution, but also, more wisdom than should be evident.

She trusted him instantly.

Slowly lowering her arm, she moved back to where the boy was standing. He took hold of her arm. She glanced at him and he gave her a weak attempt at a smile.

They waited.

Neither party made any move.

The girl could feel the boy's shuddering through his grip on her arm. She wanted to do something, anything to alleviate the impulse to act.

But she stayed, trusting the boy's words.

She trusted them more than she trusted herself.

Everything happened at once.

The wolf darted forward, startling the tense atmosphere.

She moved before she could think.

"No!" yelled the boy. She didn't hear.

His voice was drowned out by the screaming impulse inside her to protect him.

The wolf let out a howl, lunging for her.

She screamed, lunging for it.

There was a deafening sound.

And then there was the scrape of flesh.

And the pounding of fur.

There was pain.

And there was blood.

There was a hand dragging her away.

It was warm and familiar.

So she let it.

Her arm was wet. She lifted it to find three short gashes from her elbow.

She felt a shift in the ground. Her eyes flew to the boy. The girl gasped.

Beneath his foot, a small crack had formed. It bolted to where the wolf was running towards them.

The crack settled under its weight.

There was a frightful shudder and the ground around it vanished. The wolf gave a deafening howl as it plummeted, disappearing in a cloud of earth and dust.

A moment of silence passed, the boy breathing heavily, the girl trying to register what had just happened.

The boy turned to look at her, his already pale face growing paler as he saw the gashes on her arm.

"Are you okay?" he yelped, rushing towards her. She pulled her arm away, still dazed.

"I'm fine. It's only a scrape."

She surveyed the area, her eyes lingering over the hole which had just been created.

There was no sign of the wolf.

If her eyes hadn't been deceiving her, then...

She turned her gaze to the boy, who looked equally as confused as she did.

His eyes widened in shock and his mouth opened in slight.

"Madison?" he simply said.

This was enough to dumbfound her.

The boy had a similar look on his face, but he was staring at her with something other than surprise. Was it excitement? Happiness?

Relief?

"Madison..." he repeated, his eyes wide and glossy. The girl stared back, a broken smile forming on her face.

Was that her name? Before, it didn't matter to her that she knew so little about herself, or her life.

But now that she had regained something...

She needed more.

"Jason" she said.

Something flickered inside her as she said his name out loud.

She remembered nothing, but now she had feelings. So many emotions flooded into her looking at somebody she knew, somebody she loved, and her smile grew wider.

Tears pricked the corners of his eyes as they grabbed each other, laughing and smiling.

The hug was warm and familiar.

Like nothing had ever changed.

It most definitely had.

But that didn't matter to her at the moment.

Madison was just glad that no matter what happened, something, someone in her life would always be constant.

* * *

You sit on a chair at the end of the hallway.

The lamplight is dim, casting dark shadows down the length. There are no windows.

You're covered in scratches and bruises, hair flying in all directions. Your limbs are shaking, fists clenched into the handles of the chair.

You thirst for another fight.

You were weak, and unprepared. You were weak, and they got you.

Next time, they won't see it coming.

You'll show them all.

But now you're seeing red. Red, more red and a tiny hint of blue.

You'll show them.

Shaking all over, you get up from your chair, pacing wildly.

You'll show them, you'll show them, there's red, so much red and some blue and you need to hit something, hurt someone, and-

The chair is picked up and thrown across the room with a roar.

You're out of control, and you like it like that.

This way, they won't be able to hurt you as much.

This way, you can fight back.

You're ready to show them, to show them all. A dark shadow is cast down the hall, and you turn, ready to fight.

You stop suddenly, a wave of relief rushing over you. You calm down.

Seeing your state, Jason rushes over to you.

"Madison" he says, staring at you worriedly.

You look from Jason, to the chair lying on the floor.

You wait for him to connect the dots.

It doesn't take long.

He always knows when something's up, sometimes before you do.

"Are you okay?"

This question catches you off guard. It's been a while since anyone's asked you that.

In a moment of truth, you shake your head. Jason looks at you, not with pity, but understanding.

You love him even more because you know he really does understand.

"Was it a fight?"

You nod.

"Did you start it?"

Silence. You nod again.

"Do you want to tell me why?"

You stare at the ground.

"They were making fun of us."

Jason frowned, a sight you never liked seeing on his face.

"You know you shouldn't pay them any attention."

A spark lights inside you again, as you remember.

Every hit, every insult, every word.

You feel your anger growing again.

"That's hard to do when they won't ever leave me alone."

"I know it's hard. But you're better than that."

Your head droops. Your actions earlier said otherwise.

"How do you know that?"

Jason brings your head back up and you're looking into his eyes.

"Because I know you, and they don't. At least, not really."

The sight of Jason's face is enough to bring a slow smile to your lips.

Jason slumps down on the floor with you. You both watch the flickering lights, not saying a word.

"I wish we had windows here" you say.

"Why?"

"I want to see the stars."

Jason chuckled, an adorable yet annoying sound to hear.

"You know you wouldn't be able to see them. It's too dark."

You sucked in a breath, suddenly feeling stifled by the narrow hallway.

"It's almost bedtime. You need to go."

Jason stood up with you.

"You're still on your punishment. I'll wait with you."

You felt a smile form on your lips. It wouldn't be much of a punishment if he was there. Jason never failed to cheer you up.

You both sit down again, finding comfort in each other's presence.

You meant it. You really wanted to see the stars.

No. In fact, you wanted to go outside, leave this dreadful place forever.

You made up your mind. You'd leave with Jason. Leave everything, everyone behind.

There's got to be something better out there, right? And who better to do it with than the only person you care about?

Yeah.

That sounded like a plan.

CHAPTER 2

MADISON WAS AWED.

The ocean spread out in a vast expanse in front of her, colliding in gentle waves. A glittering array of sand covered the shore, shining like diamonds under the sun's rays. It rose up in a slope, converting to grass. The sky melded together in hues of pink, violet and a glowing ball of orange.

"Nice, isn't it?" Jason remarked, walking forward with a bundle of sticks. Madison smiled, wishing that the rest of her life could be like this. She could already imagine it.

Sitting on the sand watching sunsets, splashing in the ocean, lighting fires at night.

That reminded her.

The fire.

Starting one was harder than she thought. Her patience

wore thin as she rubbed two sticks together ferociously, but to no avail. Her forehead creased in concentration. Jason watched her, his grin growing the more she struggled.

He held out his hand to her, gesturing for the sticks.

"Can I try?" he asked, unable to hide his smile.

Madison didn't reply, dourly handing him the sticks. Jason got to work.

He picked the stick with the sharpest point out of the pile on the ground and began carving a line through one of the bigger logs. Madison watched with rapt attention as he continuously rubbed them together, gradually creating smoke. He added the smouldering ashes created from this to a mound of grass in his hand and waved it around in the air, presumably to let oxygen into it.

The grass eventually caught fire, and Jason threw it on the mound of sticks.

The fire blazed to life in front of them.

Madison could only stare, disbelief and awe showing on her face. "No way." She gaped at the fire's flickering form.

"Yeah, I know. I'm amazing."

Madison gave him a light thump on the arm, imitating his voice in a high- pitched tone.

The two huddled close to the fire, facing the ocean. Madison watched it, lost in the rhythmic movement of the waves on the sand. Jason faced the horizon, his face glowing with the last few rays of sunlight before nightfall. His countenance bore the semblance of a frown, just enough to show that his thoughts were troubled, whatever they were.

Madison noticed.

"What's wrong?" she asked, though she already knew the answer. Jason looked at her, and the sadness in his eyes deepened. "This whole situation is so weird."

"You think?!"

He rolled his eyes, continuing on. "Just think about it- we both find ourselves on an island with no idea how we got here and no way of finding out. And to top that off, we don't remember anything at all, but at one look, we both regain a single memory, which honestly just gives us more questions than answers, and nothing really useful to our current situation."

He turned his gaze down to his knees. Madison watched, frowning in concern as his hands began to shake and a frightened look crossed his face.

"What if we're never able to find a way back? What if we can't do anything but sit here and slowly –"

"That's enough."

Jason blinked up at Madison fearfully.

"If we keep on thinking like that, we'll never get anywhere. Sure this is all scary and stuff, but it's definitely something we can get through. But if you loose your head, you won't. Simple as. Besides, I don't even think I want to leave." She ruffled his head gently.

"Get yourself together, will you?"

Jason didn't speak, staring at Madison with wide eyes.

He managed a small smile. "Yeah...sorry about that. I haven't even been here for long and I'm already starting to loose my mind."

That caught Madison's interest.

"How long have you been here?"

"I woke up here earlier on today."

"Me too."

Jason looked at her in surprise. "Really?"

She nodded.

She hadn't really had the sense to question her situation from the beginning. She had been too immersed in her surroundings. But now that she has, nothing made sense.

A cold breeze blew in her direction, and she shuddered involuntarily, huddling closer to the fire.

"The wolf" Jason continued, a note of uncertainty in his voice. Madison felt her pulse quicken at the mention of it.

"Did you...notice anything unusual about it?"

"Like what ?" she asked. Jason shifted in his position.

"It was mostly its behaviour. Wolves generally travel together in packs, but this one was completely on its own. They normally only attack people when they feel threatened. In most cases it's when something directly assaults them. You didn't do anything, but it came for you."

He looked her in the eyes.

"A normal wolf would back down if you stayed completely still and unthreatening to them. In our case, it ignored this completely."

Madison considered this fact, her unease growing. So that's why Jason had asked her not to attack.

"What are you implying from this?"

Jason was silent for a moment.

"I'm not sure."

Silence once again took over.

The night had rolled in over the beach, bringing with it all the silence of the universe. The air was still, calm and reassuring. The sky transformed into an infinite expanse of black, millions of white dots compensating for the lack of light. The sea glistened, a mirror for the moon. A faint spell of wind brushed against the water's surface, ruffling its stillness, and rippling the moon's reflection.

The quiet gave Madison the time she needed to address all the questions that were swirling around in her mind.

There was one question that bugged her the most. "So…care to explain what it was that you did earlier on?" she murmured quietly, staring at the ground. Jason tensed, avoiding eye contact with her. He shifted uncomfortably in his spot.

"You mean the…?" he faltered, unsure of what to call it. Madison nodded.

Jason's green eyes dulled in the hazy light of the fire.

"I've been trying to figure it out since it happened, and I still haven't come up with an answer. I have no idea how I'll begin to try explain it to you."

He brought his gaze up to the smouldering flames in front of him, the light illuminating his pale and tired face.

It was then that Madison realized how much this entire ordeal was really affecting him. She compared the boy in front of her to the kind, smiling little boy that stayed with her in her memory. They hardly seemed like the same person.

"How do I put this..?" Jason narrowed his eyes in concentration, trying to find the right words.

"I don't know what to call it. But it was kind of like… a sense. An instinct in my mind told me what to do and before I knew it, I was stomping my foot on the ground and…" Jason stopped. There was no need for him to continue.

He stared at his hands in a dazed manner.

"The thing is, it felt so natural. So I must have done it sometime before I lost my memory as well."

An unsettling silence took over when he finished.

Madison sneaked a glance at Jason, and her heart squeezed terribly. He looked so...*sad*.

Without warning, she pulled him into a tight hug.

"Whatever it was, it was awesome."

Jason's eyes widened in shock, then he laughed softly as he returned it. "What was that for?" he asked teasingly when she pulled away.

"You needed a hug."

Jason smiled, the sight filling her with content.

"You're right. I did."

She lay down, gazing at the moon and billions of stars dotting the sky.

"Where do you think we came from?" Jason's small voice was heightened in the tranquility of their surroundings. Madison sighed.

"Don't know. But it mustn't have been very nice if I don't miss it."

Jason snickered.

"I should've expected that from you. But aren't you curious to find out?"

"No."

Madison's answer was final as she focused her attention to the night sky.

The twinkling of the stars were a good distraction, and enchanting. Some looked as if they flickered away, yet they always returned. Madison found herself tiring quickly, her eyes slowly starting to droop.

"Madison?" Jason's quiet voice came from beside her. Her eyes flickered open.

"Yeah?"

"Thanks."

"For what?" she asked sleepily.

There was silence for a moment, then came the quiet response.

"For being here."

Madison felt the edges of her lips tug into a smile before drifting off to sleep.

CHAPTER 3

THE ONLY SURE WAY TO ESCAPE WAS TO LEAVE SILENTLY, in the dead of
night, without making a sound.

From there, they would gain distance from the building and
be long gone before anyone even realized they were missing.

That was the initial thought going through Madison's mind,
as she packed her bag.

A sigh escaped her as she gathered the last of her scarce
belongings. She had stacked up on extra "All in One" packets
from numerous mealtimes. Nobody seemed to like the infusion
of protein, carbohydrates, water and fat, and there was always
a large stack of leftovers at the end of each meal. It may not
have been quality food, but it was better than nothing.

She grabbed a small knife off her bed, putting it in her pocket.
She'd been preparing for this day for several weeks, and she
still wasn't sure what had prompted her to do it.

She suspected that the idea came to her over a year ago when Jason had stayed with her in the hallway after she got into trouble.

It was ages ago, but she remembered vividly the strong yearning in the pit of her stomach, how desperately she wanted to leave, the way her hatred of this place and everyone in it grew.

Slinging her bag on her back, she walked to the door, not even giving her room one last look. She could already picture it in her mind. Bed at the wall, wardrobe in the corner, cupboard beside the bed. Nothing interesting or exciting.

It had served as more of a jail cell than a living space.

As silently as she could, she lifted the door handle, and peaked around the door. Nobody lurking around.

Still cautious, she slinked past the door, and shut it, barely making a sound.

Madison turned her gaze to the dark hallway. It was even more foreboding than normal, the lamps casting eerie shadows down the hall.

It sent chills down her spine.

She soundlessly made her way past several more hallways, down a flight of stairs and onto the ground floor, praying that no guards would come at that moment.

They had decided on meeting at the library, a relatively unused area in the building. Most days it seemed like she and Jason were the only ones that went there. Jason spent much more time there than she did. All he ever seemed to do was read.

Madison opened the door, taking in the familiar smell of old books and settling dust.

Now that she was there, the anxiousness left her, excitement taking over.

She couldn't wait to get out of the building, to go and explore the world outside. Failure wasn't an option for her tonight.

She preoccupied herself with flipping through some books. It slightly annoyed her that she couldn't make sense of the lines and squiggles, but overall, it was a good distraction.

Time passed, and she began to feel anxious.

What if Jason got caught before he was able to make it?

Her worry dissipated when the library door opened, Jason's outline visible.

"Sorry I'm late."

Madison looked at him expectantly.

"Did you find the guard?"

He nodded.

"Sleeping. He always does on his shift."

"I always knew his laziness would be his downfall. Let's go before he wakes up."

"Right."

She couldn't see his face in the darkness, but she could clearly see his jittery outline.

"Are you ready?" she whispered.

A grin spread on his face.

"Yeah" he whispered back.

As silently as they came in, they exited the library, closing the door firmly behind them.

They took off, making their way towards the black double doors at the entrance. The only noise to be heard was the rhythmic tap of their feet on the ceramic floor.

The area was completely vacant, so Jason risked a question.

"How far are we going?" he whispered.

Madison looked at him, a knowing glint in her eye. She had it *all planned out.*

There was a city she'd heard about.

It was full of unusual people, people just like them, who had powers.

That would be their end destination.

But for now, they'd travel and explore.

There was a whole wide world to see. And she wasn't going to stay here without witnessing any of it.

"I was thinking. We should focus on getting as far away from here as we can. Then tomorrow, we can-"

"What do you mean, tomorrow?"

Jason stopped in his tracks. He'd forgotten to whisper.

His voice echoed down the hall.

"Keep it down!" Madison hissed, her eyes darting around wearily.

Jason gave her a look.

"We're only going out for the night, aren't we?" he asked cautiously.

Madison tensed, turning around to look at him.

"I never said that."

She noticed he hadn't brought any bags with him. Jason made the same realization as her, his eyes widening.

"Do you think we're running away?" he asked. Madison's muscles tensed.

"You know it's been the plan from the start. Now let's get going. We've made enough noise by now."

She walked forward, but stopped abruptly when Jason didn't follow.

"I'm not running away" he said firmly.

Madison felt the room grow a hundred times colder.

"What?"

"You heard me. It wouldn't work out. We won't be able to last out there on our own. There's so much we don't know." Jason glared, waiting for Madison to say something. He began to worry when she didn't.

Then he noticed her trembling hands, curled into fists at her sides.

"So you think it's okay to just spend the rest of our lives here? Without ever seeing the world once?" she whispered, a deadly edge to her voice. Jason's eyes widened, shocked by the intensity of her tone.

"I never said that. I meant-"

"That's what it sounded like to me!" Madison shouted, forgetting to keep her voice down.

Jason shrank back at her heated words.

"Of course I don't want to spend my life here! But we need to be logical. The people here take care of us, give us what we need to survive. What we need is always more important than what we want." He stared her in the eye, trying to persuade her.

Madison raised an eyebrow. Of course he couldn't sway her opinion. Not on this.

"We could have what we want and need at the same time. Let me ask you this. Do they care about what we want? No, they don't. If they really did, Jason, they'd treat us like normal human beings, the way they treat the rest of the kids."

"Maybe they have a good reason for not letting anyone leave" he murmured.

"I seriously doubt that. Let's face it. The only reason they won't let us go is because they're scared of our-"

"Who's that!" a new voice shouted.

Madison froze, her heart fluttering in her chest. Jason snapped to his senses, grabbing her hand.

"What are you doing! We can't let him see us!"

Madison finally realized what was happening, and the pair began to run.

"Wait! Where are you going?!" the voice called again.

Madison heard footsteps following them down the hall. She mentally cursed herself.

If she hadn't given them away by shouting down the hall like a complete idiot, they could have been out of here by now.

It would've been perfect. Nobody would have even realised they were gone until they were unreachable. The corners of her vision blurred with a bright blue, and she tried to calm herself down.

They reached a sideway, panting heavily. Jason peaked around the corner.

"He's not following us anymore. What should we do?"

He didn't get an answer.

He glanced back at Madison.

"What're you doing?"

Madison stared at her hand, a crooked smile spreading on her face. Bright blue dust spiralled out of her palm, the particles losing their faint glow as they emerged.

"We can use our powers to take care of the guard, then run away. Nobody would know what happened, and by the time they figure out it was us, we'd be long gone."

Jason shuddered.

"I already told you. I'm not running away. And we can't use our powers, either. Especially not mine. And we were way too loud, so others must have heard us too-"

Just as he said that, more footsteps thundered behind them, maybe two or three more, with varied cries of 'Get them!', and 'Don't let them get away!'

Jason grabbed her hand and they began running again. Madison took a sharp intake of breath, doubling her speed.

Now she realized how unrealistic her plan was.

This was all a terrible idea. She stole a glance behind her, and was filled with dismay to see their pursuers steadily closing the distance between them.

What was the point of running if they were going to get caught anyway? She glanced at Jason, who was panting hard, struggling to keep up. She shouldn't have dragged him into this.

A voice of reason crept its way into her conscience, and she knew what she had to do. This was her idea, so Jason shouldn't have to face the consequences.

She gripped Jason's hand and pulled him in close enough to whisper in his ear.

"Run as fast as you can. No matter what, don't let them see your face." Jason looked at her, wide eyed and confused. "What are you talking about?" he asked. She took a deep breath, regret and sorrow laced in her voice. "I'm sorry."

Using as much strength as she could muster, she slung her arm forward, slinging Jason ahead, giving him momentum and speed.

Madison skidded to a stop, turning to face her pursuers.

Upon seeing her face, some of them slowed their pace, one stopping outright.

"She's the transcender child, isn't she?" one guard asked.

"Yeah. We need to be careful with her. They can be pretty dangerous."

"Exactly! They shouldn't even be here! They're a danger to the other kids."

Madison bristled at their words.

People were all the same.

They never really cared about you, your interests or your life.

They either needed you for something or didn't want you at all.

"Hey kid," one guard called, "If you go back to your room, we could forget that all this happened. Just don't try it again."

He stood there, waiting for Madison to follow his orders. Madison glared back at him.

What he had just suggested was the last thing she wanted. If she was honest, she would rather face the consequences then go back.

He tapped his foot impatiently on the ground.

"Well?" he asked, anger hinting in his voice.

She took a step forward. Her palms were sweaty and her heart thudded violently in her chest, but she didn't let them see her weakness.

At her step forward, the others took a step back.

"She looks like she's gonna try and pull something" one of the other guards called, fear lacing his voice.

An odd shudder went through Madison.

She was aware of the fear in everyone's faces. Were they really that scared of her? It thrilled her to an extent, but it also made her uneasy. Did they really think she was some kind of monster?

The guard who had spoken against her began to lose patience, shaking from anger.

"I've had enough of your nonsense! We should just report you and have you banished from here!" he bellowed.

Madison didn't waste any more time.

Quickly steeling herself, she ran forward and landed a quick blow to his stomach.

It wasn't exceedingly hard, but it was enough to double him over in surprise and a bit of pain. "What's wrong with you?!" he grunted, hunched over. Madison stared him down, glee showing in the depths of her wild eyes.

She was surprised at how much she had enjoyed it.

Maybe you are the monster everyone seems to think you are, whispered a little voice in her head.

She ignored it.

For now she would focus on her main goal. Getting Jason out of this safely. She sneaked a glance behind her to see if he was gone.

To her dismay, she found he hadn't left the corridor, staring at the scene with wide eyes. The distraction was all the guard needed to punch Madison in the gut, winding her and sending her sprawling on the ground. She heard Jason shout her name, and feet rushing towards her.

The world was spinning. She felt queasy, weak and helpless, unable to do anything. The last of her hope left her as she closed her eyes, waiting for the tears to come.

They didn't.

She was vaguely aware of Jason standing over her still body, challenging anyone who dared to come near. She heard a lone voice, clear and distinct amidst the current noise.

"Normally I'd have a problem with hurting little kids, but monsters don't count, right?" the voice joked.

Anger swelled in her chest, winning out over fatigue and fear.

Madison shakily stood to her feet, hearing resounding gasps from the people around her as she did so.

"We're not monsters" she growled out, a dangerous edge in her tone.

Blue tinted her vision. Little tendrils of blue dust rose out of her fingertips, letting loose in spirals. She vaguely wondered if she was hallucinating.

The voice whispered in her head, reverberating in her mind.

Show them what you can do.

And she did.

Spreading her arms, she allowed the resonating energy from her body to seep into her fingertips, the tendrils of dust rising in quantity. A collective shout rose up from the guards, realising what she was about to do.

"Get her! Before she finishes!" one of them shouted. Two of them rushed towards her, intending to take her down. Jason was in front of her in a flash, shouting something she couldn't hear at them. She felt a sudden pang of guilt at his resolve to protect her.

No longer stalling, she stretched her arms out to their full length.

A strange yet familiar feeling flooded through her fingers, creating more blue dust. It whizzed around her, full of energy. Soon there was enough of it to fill a good portion of the corridor.

The guards stopped, shielding their eyes from the flying particles. Madison drew her arms in front of her, pointing her fingers at the guards in front of her.

Everything happened at once.

The dust soared past her and Jason towards the guards, collectively glowing with an abundance of energy and power. They yelled fearfully as it swarmed around them, coating them in blue and causing them to stagger backwards, flailing on the floor. She and Jason watched the scene in front of them, eyes wide at what Madison had caused. The blue tint faded from her eyes, as did the glow from her fingers. The rush of power she felt just a second ago disappeared, leaving her feeling drained and exposed.

It never ceased to amaze her when she found the rare opportunity to use her power. Glancing over at Jason, she knew he felt the same way.

Then she felt an alertness tug at her, and realised they should leave before the dust lost its power. Already it was losing its glow, which meant energy was dissipating from it.

"Let's go" she tugged at Jason's shirt. He nodded at her. They were about to leave when a voice rose from behind them.

"Not bad, for someone who's out of practice, but you definitely need a lot of work. I mean, what's a bit of dust going to do to anyone?"

Madison whipped around, facing the intruder, but finding no one.

She never recalled hearing that voice anywhere before. She took a few steps back in her haste to keep some distance, and collided with something on the floor, landing with a thud. A hand gripped around her ankle.

"I think that's more than enough trouble for one night" the guard remarked.

"Get off!" Madison yelled, struggling with all her might, but most of her strength was already spent.

Jason watched with mounting horror and anger. He made to move towards her, but Madison wasn't having it.

"Just go! I can deal with this myself!" she shouted.

He looked between her, the guard gripping her leg, and the others recovering from the dust storm.

His eyes glistened with unshed tears, and after hesitating for a second, took off running down the corridor.

"I'm not leaving you! I'll be back!" he called. Madison looked around her. The dust had lost its glow and was getting dimmer and dimmer, falling off the guards like grains of sand.

One of them took a device out of her pocket, and held it to her ear, starting to talk.

She's getting reinforcements.

Madison felt herself slump over in defeat. There was no escaping this place. She was foolish to ever think that she could.

A tingling sensation came over her whole body.

In a flash, the strange tingling became a painful searing, starting at her feet and working its way up. It didn't take long to reach her brain, and it took all her strength to hold in her scream. Her mind went blank as her entire body spiralled out of control. Luckily, the feeling only lasted two seconds, and she was lying on the ground again. But it felt… different. She looked up, and realised she was in an entirely different room altogether.

"What?!"

She jumped up, looking around frantically. She was in a bedroom with similar traits to her own, a small space with few furnishings.

Her senses peaked when she felt a presence near her.

"A thank you would be nice. I didn't have to do this, you know" somebody drawled, stepping in front of her. Instinctively, she backed away, drawing in ragged breaths. It was the same voice that she had heard before. But at least now she could match a face to it.

He was old, but the only things that gave that away were his white hairs and the wrinkles lining his forehead. He was tall and lean, with rather broad shoulders and crinkling grey eyes. He wore a white collared shirt, rolled up at the sleeves, black trousers and polished black shoes. A well groomed moustache bloomed just below his nose, and his shoulder length white hair was drawn into a loose ponytail at his nape.

Madison stared him down, not showing an inch of the fear she felt on her face.

"Who are you?! And what just happened?" she demanded, giving him her most threatening glare yet. The old man sighed discontentedly.

"I knew it would go something like this."

He stepped forward, holding out his hand for her to shake, but Madison took another step back.

"Who are you?!" she repeated, this time a hint of fear wavering in her tone. The man halted, and some of the stiffness in his mannerism faded, the harsh look on his face melting.

"I don't really have a name. Well, I must have had one, once upon a time. But I can't remember."

Madison gave him an unimpressed look, narrowing her eyes.

"Don't treat me like an idiot. How can anyone just forget their name? If you're going to tell me a lie, at least tell me a convincing one."

The old man stared at her in surprise for a minute. Then, to her confusion, he burst out laughing.

"You really are perceptive! Sorry about that, just testing you out." His expression took a serious turn.

"I'm afraid I can't tell you my name. Not yet, anyway." Madison raised an eyebrow, her expression darkening.

"Then I guess I can't tell you mine either."

In a flash of silver, she whipped out the small knife she had kept in her pocket, brandishing it dangerously in front of him.

She had kept it with her all this time, in case the need to use it arose. She'd really wished she wouldn't have to.

"I'll give you ten seconds to start explaining how you brought me here," she explained in a dark undertone. She brought the hilt of the knife closer to his face. "Or you're going to start getting very familiar with this knife."

The old man looked alarmed at her display, but not for the reason she expected.

"Goodness, child! That's not how you hold a knife! And it's blunt, at that! You should sharpen your knife more often, especially since it's not made from a strong metal. And if you ever bring a knife to someone, you should always have them backed into a corner, so they have nowhere to run. Just some tips." he pointed out helpfully.

Madison dropped the knife to her side, disbelief showing on her face.

"You're joking..." she choked out.

The old man shook his head solemnly.

"I'm afraid I'm not, unfortunately."

He sighed, raking a hand through his hair and stifling a yawn. "As for how I brought you here, I'd say the answer is pretty obvious already. Wanna guess?"

Madison felt her whole body go rigid for a second.

"You...have powers?" she questioned, quietening her voice for some reason. The old man nodded.

She scrutinized him closer. Apart from Jason, he was the only other person with powers she had ever met.

"Now that I answered one of your questions, you can answer one of mine. What were you and your blonde haired friend doing that caused all that ruckus in the first place?" he enquired. Madison, felt her head droop at the thought of Jason and their failed escape plan.

"We… were trying to escape. But we had a little disagreement, and somebody heard us." She stared at the floor.

Why was she telling him that? She still didn't trust him, and didn't intend to.

The old man whistled upon hearing that. "That's a bad idea. A really bad one. It would be in your best interest to never try anything like that again" he warned, taking a serious tone again.

She felt her hands squeeze into fists. She knew it had been a bad idea. But from the way the old man phrased it, it sounded like she should never try to leave.

Did that mean that the ones in charge actually had a valid reason for not letting them go outside?

"Now, revisiting your earlier question…" the old man started. An array of footsteps from outside the room could be heard getting closer to them, but the old man ignored them. "I've come here for a very urgent reason, and I cannot stress to you the importance of what I want you to do."

Madison straightened up, watching him attentively. He had completely captured her attention now.

"How important?" she asked, eyes narrowed. The old man paused for a moment, twirling the end of his moustache in thought. "It has the potential to be life- changing" he decided. Madison tried not to show it, but she was tingling with anticipation and slight suspicion. She was well aware this could be some kind of trap. People rarely did things from the goodness of their hearts, in her experience.

"What is it?" she asked.

The door was thrust open, making Madison jump.

In rushed Jason, panting heavily, and collapsing against the doorframe. The footsteps were getting farther away, and she absently noted that there were more voices than there were last time.

So the reinforcements came.

She rushed towards the boy, quickly supporting his small leaning frame.

His face was bright red, and his normally neat hair was dishevelled. He collectively went through confusion, surprise and relief to find himself being supported by Madison.

"I thought you were still in the corridor. How did you escape and get here so quickly?" he asked when he finally had enough breath to speak.

Madison looked over to the strange old man, and Jason's eyes followed, widening considerably. It looked like he hadn't noticed him before.

"Who's he?" he whispered into Madison's ear.

The old man was watching them, barely holding back his look of amusement. Madison sent him an angry glare, daring him to interrupt, but that only made him chuckle quietly. She sighed and turned to Jason.

"He's the one who brought me here. I don't know who he is, or why he saved me." She leaned in closer to whisper in Jason's ear. "But get this. He has powers, like ours."

Madison thought Jason's eyes were going to pop out of their sockets. He sneaked a glance over at the man.

"Are you sure he's not lying?"

"He used his power to bring me here, so definitely not."

"How did he do that?"

"I'm not sure. He must have used-"

"You know, It's rude to talk about people behind their backs" the man interrupted, taking a step towards them. He didn't bother to hide the wide grin on his face. Madison glowered at him.

"And you know it's rude to interrupt people's conversations, so I guess we're even."

Jason stared at her in mortification, while the old man burst out laughing for the second time.

"You have a point there" he admitted.

He noticed Jason's staring at him apprehensively.

"Hello" Jason said quietly, giving the man a strange stare, one which Madison understood was calculated and purposeful. To Jason, everything and everyone was a puzzle which could be solved with patience and observation.

This came as a surprise to the old man. He had expected a reaction similar to Madison's from him.

"Hello there" he smiled warmly, ignoring Madison's threatening glare.

"What's your name?"

"James" Jason replied, not missing a beat.

Madison gave him a strange look, and the old man nodded.

"Very nice to meet you" he said, offering his hand for Jason to shake. He took it hesitantly.

He didn't show it, but he was very impressed by this boy. He knew he couldn't trust him yet, so he avoided giving him any useful information.

It would be nice to get them both on his side quickly, to avoid any more misconceptions.

"You still haven't told us what it is you want yet" Madison reminded him, obviously impatient. The old man stood up.

"Ah, yes. I'd better tell you quickly. We don't have much time, by the sound of it."

The footsteps were growing closer, and it wouldn't be long

until they found them.

The man turned to the two, eyes sharp.

"I want you two to become my students. Train with me, and learn to enhance and control your powers."

His statement was met with silence.

Madison's eyes narrowed.

"We're not interested, thank you very much" she replied, obviously untrusting.

The man nodded in understanding, turning to Jason.

"What do you think?" he asked. The boy's eyebrows were furrowed in thought. It was a good idea asking him. He seemed like the type that would think logically before answering, whereas Madison didn't even stop to consider, due to her mistrust.

"I don't understand. Why did you choose us, of all people?" he finally asked.

The old man sat down on the small bed, making a loud creak as he did.

Jason may not have realised it, but that was a very complicated question. How could he explain his real reasons to them without scaring them and making them loose the little trust that they had in him? He resolved to tell half the truth.

"Well... I didn't really have much choice, since there aren't many eligible people to find. And from what I've seen, you actually need the training. Madison, there's a lot more you can do with that blue dust than just throwing it at people."

Madison gave him an alarmed look.

"I never told you my name" she commented suspiciously.

"That would be another one of my powers."

Jason fixed him with a sceptical glare.

"You mean you have more than one?" he asked.

"Not exactly. There's more ways that one could use their power than just confining it to a single thing. Of course, abilities vary from person to person. You could learn a few of these ways if you decided to train with me." he answered.

Madison glanced at Jason to exchange a look, but he didn't spare her a glance. He stared straight ahead, eyebrows furrowed. Madison knew that look. It meant he was deep in thought, probably on the verge of figuring something out.

But she, on the other hand, wasn't convinced.

"I don't believe it. If you want me to become your student, you'll have to show me what you can do. Words mean nothing to me" she declared, staring the man straight in the eye. He sighed in irritation.

"Very well. If I must."

He turned to the door, eyes hardened. The sound of feet beating against the ground and muffled shouts were getting unbearably loud.

His whole demeanour changed. Facing towards the door, an air of forcefulness surrounded him.

"Stand back. You want to see proof of my power? Well, I'm about to show you."

"But-" Jason tried to object. At that moment, the door flew open, and a crowd of people rushed into the room, armed with rifles and shields.

More guards.

Madison and Jason ducked behind the old man, fear taking over them.

I'd like to see how he can get us out of this situation, Madison thought.

"Sir, get away from those two quickly! They're extremely dangerous!" a woman at the front of the group spoke. The old man took a step forward, something unrecognisable glinting in his eyes.

"I don't see how two children could be dangerous to a group of armed adults. I believe it's all of you who should leave."

That statement was met with shocked mutterings and whispers. Madison noticed that the man's fist was closed at his side, but upon closer inspection, she saw a faint golden glow come from it. Jason noticed it too, and exchanged a confused look with her.

It was evident now that the old man had some kind of power. But how would it help them right now?

A guard in the front also noticed the old man's glowing fist. It was getting brighter, and Madison could even faintly feel heat radiating off it. Little by little, her fear chipped away to curiosity and excitement. Just what was this man planning to do?

The guard in the front paled quickly when he realised what he was planning.

"Secure them all immediately! He's trying to protect them because he's one of them as well!"

Madison and Jason watched as the guard's expressions collectively went from surprise, to anger and fear. In a split second, all their guns were trained on the three.

But they never got the chance to shoot. The man lifted his arm, and Madison briefly noticed an elaborately tattooed M in cursive font just below his elbow. With a quick snap of his fingers, a strong wave resonated throughout the room, the force of it causing Madison and Jason to shield their eyes. Madison looked back up again. None of the guards moved an inch. Then it occurred to Madison that they had been frozen still.

Any ounce of doubt she once felt had vanished completely.

This was real. He truly did have powers.

The old man wrung out his arm, and turned to face the both of them.

"Was that enough proof for you?" he asked Madison, a hint of sarcasm in his tone. She found herself unable to say anything, so she nodded silently. She glanced over at Jason, curious of his reaction.

He stood rigidly, eyes wider than Madison had ever seen them before. "What's wrong?" she asked worriedly. He ignored her completely, his eyes focused on the old man. Madison knew that whatever Jason had been puzzling out before, he had just figured out.

"You're a Master" he blurted out, pointing at the old man. Madison watched him in surprise.

"A what?"

The old man stared at Jason, impressed.

"I knew you were clever, but I never imagined to this extent. How'd you figure it out?"

"Your mark. I read about it in a book I found in the library."

The master lifted his elbow, showcasing the cursive M Madison had spotted before.

"I also got a bit suspicious when you said you could use your power in different ways. I read that it requires a lot of training, though I thought you could have been lying about that part. But it was obvious when I saw you use your power. I can't believe-"

"Can someone just answer my question? What the hell is a Master!?" Madison interrupted loudly, looking between the two with an annoyed glare. Jason rolled his eyes and sighed before answering.

"I told you about it before, remember? A transcender who

has reached the peak of power." Jason's eyes were alight, staring at the Master with excitement and admiration.

"But I never thought that one would actually still exist. And to think we'd get to train with one..." he trailed off, his smile growing wider. The old man smiled fondly at Jason.

"I see you've already made your decision. What about you, Madison?" he asked her quizzically.

Her choice was already made. If Jason wanted to train with this Master, she had to go too. Someone had to look after him. Besides, maybe this training could be her ticket out of there someday. Despite the Master's warning, she was still intent on leaving. Anywhere was better than this prison for Madison.

"Yeah, sure. Whatever" she replied, feigning indifference to the situation. Jason beamed at her, and she felt a warm feeling in in stomach. All this would be worth it if it made Jason happy.

The Master clapped his hands together loudly.

"Now that's all done and dusted, it's time for you two to go to bed. It is way past your bedtime" he stated, emphasizing the "way."

Madison sniffed disapprovingly. "We don't have a bedtime" she corrected.

Jason shook his head at her with a sigh.

"There are more important things to worry about, you know. Like how we're going to get all these guards back to where they came from" he added, glancing at the unmoving human statues. They still had their guns trained on them, and the sight sent a shiver down Madison's spine.

"Don't you worry about that. I'll take care of these guys. It'll be like nothing ever happened. All you have to worry about is getting back to bed without anyone noticing you" the old man *reassured.*

Jason nodded gratefully, and looked over at Madison.

"We should get going" he told her. She sucked in a breath, holding it in.

She didn't want to go back, not for a second.

When she'd walked out of her room, she'd truly believed it would be her last time doing so. If she went back in there, she would feel suffocated by the cramped, lifeless walls she spent a good deal of her life behind. She knew for a fact that there was something better for her out there. But now she might never be able to find it. She waited for the tears in her eyes to fall, but they didn't.

They never did.

The Master noticed, and in two quick strides, he was at her side.

Madison stared at the ground, unwilling to acknowledge his presence.

He looked down at her, pity in his thoughts.

She wouldn't be so keen to leave if she knew what was really out there.

He kneeled down, placing a hand on her shoulder. Madison didn't look up.

"There will come a time where you'll have to leave this place behind for good, and explore the world outside. But today is not that day. For now, focus on training and getting stronger for when that day comes" he spoke in a reassuring tone. Madison said nothing, but nodded gloomily, wiping her tearless eyes.

The old man stood up, satisfied that she was alright.

"You should get going now. I need to finish this up quickly."

"But when will we see you again?" Jason asked worriedly.

The Master gave him a knowing smile, and bent down to

ruffle both their heads.

"I will come whenever I come. Which will be quite often, by the way" he said with a smirk.

Madison and Jason watched the Master retreat from them with differing emotions. Jason with awe and admiration, and Madison with a strange feeling she didn't quite recognise yet, though she noted that it was a pleasantly nice one.

With a snap of the Master's fingers, the guards frozen in place had disappeared. The two children watched in amazement as the old man's form flickered, making him transparent for a split- second. His body glowed with golden light, and bit by bit, diffused into tiny golden particles.

Madison observed quietly, noting that it vaguely resembled the dust that she could create.

The diffused dust rose up into the air, and disappeared. The glow in the room faded, and the eerie dark returned. Madison looked around. Nothing there indicated that what happened had ever taken place. It was just an ordinary room now.

"That was amazing!" Jason grinned. Madison didn't show it outwardly, but she agreed.

"He's a show off" she muttered. Jason laughed at her statement, but clamped his mouth shut shortly afterwards, realizing they were meant to be quiet.

"Let's go" he whispered. Madison nodded, and they stalked out of the room silently, knowing better than to repeat past mistakes.

She closed her eyes.

And suddenly she was in a completely different place.

"Remember what I told you" *A voice spoke from the darkness.*

Buildings lay in ruins all around her. A strong gale whipped around her, chilling her to the bone. She had never experienced cold like this in her entire life.
And it was dark.
So dark.
How could anyone stand this for so long?
Jason was right next to her, struggling in in the wind. Just taking a glance at his tear- streaked face was enough for her to be reminded all over again of the horrors they had seen.
What they had done.
A gasp escaped her, and she relieved everything that happened all over again.
Those creatures were coming for them now.
She remembered when she first saw them, the fear that had gripped her.
Fresh panic took over her, and she squeezed her eyes shut, wishing for once that the voice in her head would go away, that everything *would go away.*
"Remember what I told you" the voice repeated, and Madison opened her eyes again. She couldn't see much through the wind and tears in her eyes, but she recognised the voice as the Master's.
" This is what everything has been leading up to, since the day I took you as my students."

She remembered that day over four years ago as if it had happened yesterday. But what did it have to do with what was going on now?

"I'm sorry I can't explain anything more to you, but you need to go."

Madison felt herself tense up with fear. The Master didn't sound quite like his normal self. Where was he supposing they would go, anyway?

She was about to ask him when a blinding blue light flashed underneath her, exuding energy.

She opened her eyes in shock, and she was falling. She was too surprised to scream, or make any noise. A blur of bright colours passed by her as she flailed helplessly. Through all this, a voice reverberated in her mind.

You must find the Source.

She felt her vision fading to darkness as she plummeted through the maze of colours.

* * *

You must find the Source.

Madison jolted awake with these words echoing in her mind, feeling even more lost than she had when she first woke on the island.

CHAPTER 4

So many questions.

So few answers.

Her mind was a swarm of thoughts, a nest of feelings.

And a memory. A single memory, which had managed to uproot her entire existence, and make her question her entire situation.

The girl she had been yesterday- carefree, happy and self indulgent- was a completely different person altogether.

She liked that girl better.

Everything in her mind was much simpler.

Madison questioned everything. Was the memory even a memory? Or was it just a dream?

She hoped it was the latter, but something about its familiarity, its snugness inside her mind, like it was another piece of the puzzle, made her doubt that.

Without warning, a searing pain sparked through her head, the same as the one she had gotten before, though it only lasted a second, and wasn't as sharp. Cradling her head, she sat herself up, her heart pounding in her chest.

It seemed whenever she tried to remember anything, the headache returned. She sighed.

"But more importantly," she whispered to herself, "What's the Source?"

The Source.

Thinking about it, Madison imagined a glowing golden ball fizzing with energy.

How would she find something like that on an island? What if she couldn't find it? The island was so big, it would take forever to look for.

Or what if it was all just her imagination?

More questions filled her head, piling up steadily and bringing with it a feeling of anger. The cut from the day before still thrummed with a steady ache, a reminder of the strange events.

The overbearing weight of everything was crushing her all of a sudden, and it made her feel so…helpless.

She stood up, pacing around aggressively, trying to rid her mind of all its burdens.

"What are you doing?" Jason asked, sitting up tiredly.

Madison saw him, and was instantly soothed by his image.

His hair stuck up in weird angles, his eyes half lidded and droopy as he yawned.

"Nothing" she answered, her voice calmer than her mind was.

Jason squinted at her, seeing through her easily.

"Then why were you walking around like that?"

She sighed in defeat. Nothing ever got past Jason.

"Trying to relieve some stress" she answered truthfully.

Jason didn't even seem perturbed, merely lifting an eyebrow.

"Why?" he asked.

Madison felt her senses snap.

Why? *Why?*

There were a million answers but not enough solutions to that question!

"Well let's see" she started, her tone seething, "I'm tired, I'm starving, I don't remember who I am, or anything about my life, I'm confused and lost, I have no idea why I'm here, and I had a dream-" she stopped suddenly. Jason looked fully awake now.

"A dream about what?" he asked, slowly and carefully.

Madison felt her shoulders stiffening, the memory being reinforced in her mind again.

It had felt so real. But there was still the possibility that it had just been a very vivid dream.

"It was nothing, really" she lied. Jason's brow furrowed, but he didn't enquire any further.

A loud grumble interrupted her from her thoughts. Unsurprisingly, it had come from her stomach.

That alerted her to another problem.

"What're we going to eat?" she asked.

Neither of them knew how to fish or hunt, and she wasn't exactly an expert at distinguishing between edible and inedible plants.

Jason stopped for a moment, seeming to remember

something.

"I came across a place yesterday. There was some fruit there."

This caught her attention.

"Were they edible?"

"I didn't really care when I found them, I was starving. But if it helps to know, I'm not dead now. If you really want to test-"

"Yes."

Madison hadn't realised how hungry she'd been until just now. If alleviating her hunger meant traversing through the island to find some possibly poisonous fruit, then so be it.

Jason stood up, dusting down his hoodie and jeans.

"Let's get going." he started walking, going in the direction of forest.

Madison shuddered, remembering the still uneasiness she had felt in there before the attack.

And what had resulted.

She shook her head, clearing the haziness of her mind.

She headed in. The last thing she would do was to let fear control her.

* * *

The first few minutes of travelling had spent in silence, both focused on their surroundings, and averting the questions swirling around in their minds. After that,

Madison couldn't contain them all.

"Did you remember anything about your life before you found me?"

"Nothing at all. I only got a memory when I found you yesterday."

Madison nodded, taking that in.

On they trudged, through bushes, swatting away branches and crushing twigs under their feet. She found herself tiring, even though it had only been a few minutes.

"What have you been doing since you got here?" she questioned again.

There was a stretch of silence, their footsteps echoing through the forest. Jason spoke softly.

"Just surviving, I guess. There's not much else to do in a place like this."

More silence.

"Do you remember how you made that hole yesterday?"

Jason tensed, his fingers curling into fists.

"Can we talk about something else?" he snapped. At Madison's taken-aback look, he smiled hurriedly and said, "This is more like an interrogation than a conversation. I thought you had more people skills than that."

He walked ahead, leaving Madison to gawk in his wake. She scoffed, walking back to him.

"Come on! You of all people should know that I don't have people skills. Or skills in general."

Jason raised an eyebrow.

"How can you be so sure? You've just lost your

memory, so you don't know what kind of person you were." The reminder hit hard in Madison's gut, silencing her for a second.

"I've seen enough of my memories to know that I'm not exactly the nicest to be around" she responded flatly.

Jason frowned at that.

"Why would you say that?"

Madison took a deep breath. Now was the time to tell him.

"I had a dream last night…"

And she told him what had happened in explicit detail, a dream that had felt so real, like it had actually happened. Jason was quiet the entire time, listening with rapt attention.

When she finally finished, there was a pause which felt like eternity before anyone spoke.

Madison looked at him, but didn't expect to see the utter fear on his face.

Fear found its way into her mind as well. Jason wouldn't be scared for no good reason.

"What's wrong?" she asked.

Jason fixed her with a strange haunted gaze.

"I had the same dream."

Not for the first time, Madison was rendered unable to speak.

"I…what?" she spluttered. There was nothing she could think to say. What was there to say, in a moment like this?

If that was true, then…

She grimaced as the truth hit her as suddenly as an icy cold splash of water.

It hadn't been a dream. They truly were memories.

She was sure Jason knew it too, but it seemed neither of them wanted to address it out loud.

They travelled on in silence, each wanting to be alone with their thoughts.

They were making steady progress when Jason stopped abruptly.

Madison stepped forward, frowning.

"What's –" she stopped herself, seeing for herself what was wrong.

"Oh crap."

A giant hole sat in the middle of a small clearing. Despite the difference, Madison recognised it as the hole in the ground Jason had made to save her from the wolf. It had gotten a lot bigger than before.

"What a mess" she hummed. Jason shot her a glare.

"Well, it was either that, or let the wolf tear you to shreds." Madison sighed.

"Relax, would you?"

She squinted at the hole. It was too dark to see how far down it went.

Stepping back, Madison watched Jason as he found a big rock leaning against a tree. He hauled it out, a frenzy of insects scurrying out from underneath. He lugged it over to the hole, struggling to get a strong grasp with his small hands. Madison watched, confusion evident on her face.

"What are you doing?" she asked.

Jason lugged it over to the edge, breathing heavily from the effort.

"You know that thing people do where they throw

something down a hole and count how long it takes the object to hit the ground? Same idea, but I'm using this so we can actually hear it." she shrugged lightly.

"Go ahead, then."

With that, Jason pushed the rock down the hole.

They waited…

Ten seconds turned to twenty, then thirty, then forty. Soon they had waited a full minute.

They didn't hear the rock hit the bottom.

"Holy crap" Madison muttered, eyes wide.

Jason stared, shock registering on his face.

"I did that?" he whispered, seeming unable to believe it. Madison couldn't quite believe it either.

Nothing seemed to make sense here.

"What is going on here? Yesterday, it wasn't nearly as big. But now…" she trailed off. She turned to Jason.

"How did you do it?!" she demanded.

"I told you already, I don't know how!" Jason replied back harshly, his anger mounting.

"But you should know how, since you were the one who did it!"

"You have to understand that it's not something you can just explain! Especially if you don't understand it!"

Their shouting match echoed through the forest.

"Come on! It would have to be extremely hard to create a bottomless pit without having a clue of how you did it! Look, I remember next to nothing about my life, so having at least one thing clear would really help!"

Jason closed his eyes.

"I'm going to say this one more time. I. Don't. Know. How!"

A low growl caught their attention. Madison's stomach gave a sudden lurch.

"Not again."

Jason grabbed Madison's hand, and he tugged her away.

"Hide" he whispered.

She quickly complied, ducking behind the large tree the rock had been leaning against. Jason followed suit.

The wolf prowled into the clearing, teeth bared, a deep snarl sounding in its throat. Jason's hand tightened around hers.

"Why don't you do what you did before?" she whispered to him. He shook his head.

"Did you not understand what I was screaming at you about? I don't know how."

The wolf's head snapped in their direction, and Madison's heart nearly jumped out of her chest. Jason's eyes were round as marbles, his face drained of colour.

Madison knew hiding was pointless. Standing there and wishing wasn't going to help them in any way. The wolf would find them in the end, and the inevitable would happen.

Anger welled inside her, fear temporarily forgotten.

Why should they hide, then? If her memory was correct (and it was), she should have powers, just like Jason.

So why couldn't she use them?

Because you don't know how, dummy.

Madison ignored that reason.

Her mind was set.

She stood up, letting go of Jason's hand. Before he could react, she stepped out from the tree, in full view of the

~ 63 ~

wolf.

"You wanted to find me? Well here I am. I'm done hiding, and I'm not giving in without a fight!"

All she could see was red, and her thoughts were muddled in her head.

She could feel Jason's terrified gaze burning into her back, but she ignored him. It was too late to turn back now.

The wolf was very still, sizing Madison up with narrow slit eyes. It didn't make any attempt to move. Madison felt her confidence grow.

"What? You're too scared now? I should've known you were all bark and no bite."

It probably wasn't a good idea taunting it, but she had to do something.

The tense atmosphere in the air was unnerving. It was as if the whole forest was still, watching, waiting for something to happen.

And it did.

But not what she'd expected.

"I only want the Source" a low, gruff voice spoke.

Madison nearly jumped out of her skin.

"Did it just talk?!"she spluttered. The wolf didn't answer her.

So Jason was right. This isn't a normal wolf.

Her mind was a blur, and her heart hammered inside her chest. She gulped.

"What do you mean by the Source?" she asked nervously, her voice wavering slightly.

The wolf growled, teeth bared, sharp and yellow.

"I'm not playing your games, little girl. I know you

have it."

It took Madison a second too long to answer, and as she was forming her words, the wolf sprang at her. She let out a scream, and at the last second, kicked it away from her. She landed on the ground. The wolf landed on its feet, its dark eyes seeming to have gotten stormier. Jason yelled behind her, and scrambled to help her up. The wolf took slow, small steps towards them.

"You're making this far too difficult. Just give me the Source."

Madison stood up, brushing dirt from her face. Her eyes were stormy, narrowed down with anger and hatred. Whether it could speak or not, the wolf was going to pay for that.

"I already told you. I'm not giving in without a fight." She growled, so full of menace, that even Jason flinched. He looked beyond terrified.

"Madison, I really don't think-"

A low rumbling sounded beneath their feet.

All three stopped for a minute, staring at the ground with varying looks of bafflement. With no warning or explanation, the wolf sped off, leaving Jason and Madison dumbfounded.

"What's going on? Why'd the wolf just leave like that?" Madison wondered out loud.

"He must have sensed something. This rumbling isn't normal."

It was getting louder and louder. Madison strained her ears."It sounds like it's coming from the hole" she pointed out wearily.

The forest seemed to be getting darker, the filtered sun

through the leaves vanishing.

With a pang, Madison realised that it was getting darker.

"What's going on?" Jason asked. Madison couldn't answer.

All life seemed to have departed the forest, only the eerie whispers of a cold wind staying back to haunt them.

But otherwise it was still. Madison instinctively grabbed Jason's shaking hand. Jason squeezed back hard, grateful for the comfort. She found it hard to move her legs, which appeared to be paralysed with fear.

She tried to push her unexplained feeling of unease deep down, but it just came back up, stronger than ever before.

This isn't normal, she thought frantically, trying to calm the quickening pulse of her heart, but to no avail.

But, in a sense, it all felt familiar to her somehow.

The shaking of limbs, the rising bile in her throat, a freezing gale whipping around her, the looming darkness and panic she felt.

She could hear a scream, faraway but distant in her mind.

But it wasn't hers.

No, it wasn't hers.

It was his.

As chilling and heart-breaking as it had been that day.

With eyes wider than they had ever been, she stumbled back onto the ground, brimming with surprise and grief.

Her breaths were restless and out of control as she stared out into the bleak depths that had originally been the sky.

A pair of glowing green eyes gazed back at her.

Madison felt like she could pinpoint the exact moment where her insides turned to ice, where fear, grief and pain felt like the only emotions she had ever experienced.

Looking into those eyes made her stomach feel like it was imitating the sensation of plummeting down a pitch black hole, no beginning or end in sight.

As darkness swallowed her, one last image flashed through her mind.

A streak of red hair, a smile so bright, it could replace the sun.

Then nothing.

CHAPTER 5

FEAR IS A STRONG EMOTION.

One could possibly argue that it is the strongest, the one that instantly triggers your instinct for self- preservation.

But I don't believe that for a second.

I think anger and hatred are the strongest.

Madison is living proof.

Hatred can quite easily turn to anger. It can cause you to make rash decisions without thinking twice. It can become a source of renewing energy in your body that gives you extra strength to attack and fend off enemies.

Fear causes you to run.

Anger causes you to stand up and fight.

But it is also fleeting, and one can only cling to it for so long.

Madison's ability to hold onto hatred can make her stronger, in a strange way.

I don't remember much about anything, but I remember her vividly, for some reason. It's strange. My memories are blurred, unreachable. Yet her outline is always there, right beside me, every single time.

The thing that struck me about her was her eyes.

Narrowed down into slits, brimming with hatred and a wild, animalistic rage.

That's when it occurred to me that she was strong.

And that's why it surprised and terrified me when I saw her collapse after looking into that creature's eyes.

The creature.

I hardly dared look at it, for fear that I would end up unconscious too.

I'd caught a glimpse, though.

A condensed mass of black wisps collected in the air, seeming to exude freezing gale- like winds.

I shuddered, crossing my arms around my dark hoodie.

A pair of glowing green eyes sat in the middle of the dark cloud, somehow the most terrifying part of the creature.

I noted, with concern, that it was completely ignoring me.

It came to me that it was focusing on Madison.

My heart flipped in my chest.

Fear was so dense in the air, one could probably cut it with a knife. I was shaking all over, from fear and the cold.

Move, I willed my legs, but they stayed frozen to the spot. Panic mounted in my head.

Why was I so useless? I couldn't even move to save the only person in my life from certain death.

There was only one thing I could do.

"Hey!" I tried to let out a loud, fierce bellow, but instead, my voice came out as a feeble croak.

It heard me anyway.

Faster than anticipated, the creature swung around to me, wispy black threads rising out from its dark mass.

I'd forgotten how to breathe.

The intense aura emanating from the creature was the most terrifying thing I had ever experienced. Suddenly I was suffocating in the coldness of the air, shivering violently in the freezing wind. But I didn't dare look into the creature's eyes, or I would lose the last shred of bravery I had.

Not knowing what else to do, I tried to steady my voice as best as I could, but it still came out shaky and squeaky.

"Leave us alone" I half- whispered, gazing at the floor. The creature's indefinite form stayed still, probably sizing me up.

I mentally cursed myself.

Why did I think that stupid plan would work?!

I was stuck, now.

The rest of this could play out two different ways.

The creature leaves Madison alone and comes after me. After its finished, it goes after Madison.

Or it could happen the other way around. It could ignore me and continue with Madison and go after me when its done.

Either way, we're screwed.

I found myself wondering what Madison would do in this situation.

I already knew the answer.

She would ignore all reason and charge at the creature head on. She would run forward, hatred etched onto her features, fear torn and forgotten. Perhaps she would find a way to use her powers mid- fight and defeat it effortlessly. But I definitely knew that she wouldn't cower in fear, like I was doing.

For some reason, I found myself getting angry. Perhaps it was because of Madison in my thoughts, or maybe it was the shame of my own cowardice, but my fists clenched at my sides.

What gave this creature the right to come here and pick a fight with me?! I hadn't done anything wrong, and neither had Madison.

I started to shake again, this time not with fear, or the cold.

But with fury.

I drew my hand out in front of me, full of confidence for

the first time. I stared into the creature's eyes at last. Glowing green slits gazed back at me curiously.

"Leave us alone" I spoke, my voice finally loud and steady.

The words seemed to flow out on their own, sounding completely natural being uttered by my lips.

"Go back to the nothing from which you were made."

The strangest thing happened.

The indefinite form of the creature flickered and warped continuously, until it resembled that of a man. Its new form moved towards me, taking slow, lumbering steps. It came to my feet, and crouched down low, its head bent reverently. I stared at it, terrified.

Then I realised.

It was *bowing*.

To *me*.

Some strange incomprehensible garble came out from its mouth, deep and croaky.

Just as things couldn't get any more confusing, the creature's form flickered one last time, breaking into smaller and smaller parts. Soon the particles were small enough to be compared to dust. They rose up into the black sky, disappearing from sight.

I blinked twice.

Then rubbed my eyes.

And pinched my cheek, to check that I wasn't dreaming.
Unfortunately, this was very, very real.

The surroundings changed back to their normal state
from the almost pitch- black they were before. Sunlight
shone down on my skin again, erasing any last traces of
the piercing cold that had taken over just moments ago.

But everything was far from fine.

I glanced at Madison. She lay on the floor, her breaths
deep and unperturbed.

Like nothing had ever happened.

My bravery from earlier had vanished completely, and I
felt fresh panic and fear closing in on me.

How was I going to get Madison to our destination now?

With no other options, I went over to pick her up. She
didn't weigh as much as I thought, and it was rather easy
to drape her arms over my shoulders and give her a piggy
back.

I started shakily on my way, still rattled by the
encounter.

My mind felt numb, like the creature had found a way
to reach inside my head and freeze it too.

What was that thing? How did I know what to say to
make it disappear? Or was everything that happened just
my imagination?

Not knowing anything was tearing me up from the
inside.

A thought came to my mind.

It came from the hole.

The hole I created.

So…did I..?

No.

That couldn't be possible. I have no idea how I could have done that.

It wouldn't make sense.

But, now that I think about it, nothing does here.

I don't know anything. How we got here, how we lost our memories.

How I made that hole.

A burst of pain exploded through my skull.

Oh, but I think you do know.

The voice caught me off guard.

It was deep and somehow familiar, calling to me in a sing- song tone. Clutching my head while struggling to hoist Madison up, I glanced around frantically, searching for its source.

It sounded like it was everywhere, ringing out at me from every orifice.

But it was nowhere at the same time.

I trembled, not even trying to hide my fear.

"Who are you?" I shouted out into the wind.

No need to use your outside voice when I'm inside.

The pain in my head strengthened when I heard it again. As did the pounding of my heart.

"What are you talking about?"

I think you already know. You're not as clueless as you believe you are.

"But I don't know!" my voice was desperate as I clawed at the voice for information.

"Tell me" I said, shaking all over.

I got no reply.

Glancing at my back, I saw Madison. Her head rested on my left shoulder. She didn't look peaceful even while sleeping.

In the sweltering heat of the sun, I felt almost numb. I couldn't stop the tears from leaking, and they fell, leaving the ghost of their presence lingering on my cheeks.

Was the voice real? Or was it just in my head?

Had I finally gone insane?

I lumbered through the woods towards our location again. I had to keep moving, doing something, or I'd loose the last of my motivation.

Fear was strong in my mind.

But the desperation to find all the answers was even stronger.

Knowledge is power.

And I needed to get as much of it as I could.

CHAPTER 6

Move quickly.

Don't let him touch you.

Dodge left. Dodge again. And again- the punch got you this time.

Feel it. Feel the sting, the pain, the sorrow.

The anger.

Jump out of his reach.

And attack.

Don't stop. Kick him, punch him, bite him.

Again, again, again.

Listen to his screams. Ignore the voices. Ignore them all.

"Monster!"

Ignore it. Continue.

"What is she?"

Kick, punch.

"She's out of control, that's what!"

Punch, punch. The punches get weaker.

No. You can't be weak. You need to be strong. To survive. To win.

He grabs you. You were slow. You've lost.

You feel it again. The pain, the burning anger. The punch.

Kick, kick, kick.

He throws you to the ground and the room erupts in cheers.

Something cold and metallic cuts your cheek. You can't move.

Move.

Move!

They're going to hurt you. You can't let that happen.

Move.

You stay on the ground.

Let them try hurt you. You still have some strength left. You wait, your eyes closed.

Nothing happens. You open your eyes. The room is empty.

They all left.

You tremble then. From rage, from what they said, what they did. You tell yourself not to hold back, next time.

They'll get what they deserve next time.

One comes in. They're holding a box.

You pick yourself off the ground, repeating the mantra in your head.

Don't hold back, don't hold back, don't hold back-

You don't hold back.

You feel something else, then. The feeling.

You see blue, you hear blue.

You are blue.

The room is alight with blue. With dust. You put all your

pain, all your rage into the blue. The blue feels it too.

You and the blue are one.

You aim it all at the person at the door.

You're ready, ready to become the monster they all say you are.

Then you see his face.

Everything stops.

His eyes aren't malicious, angry or even scared.

His face isn't twisted into a sneer, or white with fear.

His eyes are wide, amber reflecting the light.

His face is joyous, filled with awe.

Everything stopped.

You stopped.

The blue and the dust disappear. To nothing.

You and the blue were one.

You are nothing too.

The boy talks, but you hear nothing of what he says. He comes nearer, clutching his box. You tense.

His smile falters.

"Are you okay?"

You're surprised. Nobody's ever asked you that before. Apart from Jason. Jason was the only one you could trust.

You don't answer the boy. You stare at him, trying to make sense of him.

Challenging him.

Your eyes meet and he understands.

Without a word, he sets his box on the ground and opens it up.

He surprises you again. It's full of medical supplies. You realise you're hurt.

He wordlessly opens a bottle of liquid. The letters on it are old and faded, but that doesn't matter to you. You can't read anyway.

He pours some of the liquid in it to a small, white, fluffy material.

"This is an antiseptic. It will clean the scar on your face. It might sting a little, but I know you've handled worse. Can I put it on?" the boy asks in a tone calmer and gentler than anyone has ever spoken to you before. You put a hand to your cheek, where the metal on the ground scratched you. It comes away with tinges of red.

You don't answer again. The boy only smiles at you, and raises the white thing slowly to your face.

He's right. It does sting.

You jerk at first and tears threaten to spill from your eyes, but they don't.

They never do.

You get used to the sting. It even calms you. The pain lets you remember that you're still alive, still fighting.

He finishes and takes the white thing away from your face. It's stained red.

He takes something else out from his strange box.

A plaster. The wrapper comes off and he places it on your scar. You're shocked by how careful he is not to hurt you, how gentle his fingers are on your cheek.

He moves on next to the bruises on your arms. An oily concoction reaches your skin and makes the bruises feel like they're healed already.

You wonder if there's anything in his strange box that can heal the scars on your heart.

"What you did back there was amazing. The most awesome thing I've ever seen."

You stop again. Was he talking about the fight? You tilt your head to the side, asking a silent question.

He understands.

"I'm talking about the blue light and dust. I don't like fights."

The boy never ceases to confuse you. How can something so dangerous, so monstrous be a good thing? The blue light and dust was just anger and hatred built up to become a lethal weapon.

It could never be good.

You shake your head in disagreement.

The boy frowns. You don't like his frown. His smile is nicer.

"Why don't you like it?" he asks.

You don't answer for the longest time. Then your mouth finally opens.

"It makes me a monster."

The boy's eyes widen, probably in shock.

"I don't think you're a monster. I think your power is beautiful. When I saw it, it made me feel really happy."

Your eyes widen, entertaining the idea. Your power was beautiful? It could make people happy?

But then you saw the others, taunting you, calling you names.

Freak.

Monster.

Transcender.

Then you knew that could never be the case.

The boy sees the change in your demeanour, and understands.

He always seems to understand.

"I think the others are jealous" he declares.

You stare at him like he's a madman.

"No, seriously. They see your amazing power and wish they could be like you. I think it's incredible."

This simple comment does something strange to you.

A warm feeling fills your stomach, and you feel light-headed.

You look at the boy, searching for truth in his face.

His hair is red, tied into a short ponytail at the nape of his neck, though some has escaped and covers part of his face.

His expression is serious, not joking in the slightest, yet still kind.

But his eyes say the most.

Those eyes contain more truth, love and kindness than you've ever been shown in your entire life.

You feel an emotion similar to happiness as you realise he meant every word.

You hold out your hand.

"Madison" you say your name out quietly, but firmly.

The boy takes it gently and squeezes it.

"I already know" he says.

* * *

Madison woke to the sound of water.

Her eyes staring at the endless sky, she felt strangely at peace.

She lay there for a few moments, the lull of rushing water in her ears, thinking of the boy from her memory, his soft amber eyes and the kindness they held.

Her daydream abruptly ended when an image of the terrifying creature from before flooded into her mind.

She yelped, leaping up from her spot.

"Jason!" she screamed.

He came running almost the moment she called, dropping several indistinguishable small things from his arms as he did.

Madison finally found the sense to pay attention to her surroundings.

She let out a gasp of surprise.

They were in a large clearing. The sound of rushing water turned out to be a huge waterfall, water cascading down from the height and crashing into an endless looking blue lake.

To Madison, the body of water seemed like it could stretch on forever, but she could see tiny trees just beyond it.

Nearer to the waterfall, there were more trees and some bushes, but these bore something that reminded her of the emptiness of her stomach.

Fruit.

"Are you okay? Did something happen?" Jason finally got to her, grabbing her hands in worry and concern. She instantly snapped out of her daydream.

"Jason…what is this place? How did we get here?"

When he realised that Madison was okay, he relaxed. She could practically see the tension being released from his shoulders. He smiled in relief.

"We've arrived. This is where I was taking you. Where I found the fruit."

At the mention of fruit, Madison's eyes drifted to the

trees and bushes near the waterfall. Jason followed her gaze, and realising where it went, took something out from his pocket. Small, round and bright pink.

And very edible looking.

"What's that?" Madison asked the obvious question.

"They're some kind of fruit. I don't know what they're called, and quite frankly, don't care, as long as they're not poisonous."

Madison nodded, finding no fault with that reasoning.

Jason handed the strange pink fruit to her. Her stomach gave an impatient gurgle.

"Do they taste nice?" she asked uncertainly.

"That's for you to find out" Jason replied unhelpfully.

She gave him an unimpressed look and took a bite.

She froze.

Flavour seemed to explode in her mouth, a blend of sweetness and a strange exotic taste indulging her taste buds at the same time.

It was heaven.

She quickly swallowed, staring at the fruit in wonder.

"Holy crap! These are actually good!" she blurted out.

Jason grinned at her reaction.

"I know, right? I wouldn't even mind that much if they were poisonous."

Madison finished the rest of the fruit in a hurried frenzy, slowly gaining back some strength and energy. She grinned, her stomach giving a satisfied growl. But her throat was still feeling dry, although the pink fruit had helped a bit.

She walked over to the edge of the lake, bent down and scooped up some water with her hands. As the liquid rushed down her throat and quenched her thirst, she couldn't help but feel happy, content for once in her life.

After a few more scoops of cold, fresh water, she splashed some in her face, washing the sleep and dirt out of her features.

A movement beneath the surface of the lake made her stop and stare for a minute. The minute stretched on, but the interest had changed. She was no longer intrigued by what was beneath the surface.

But what was on it.

Her reflection.

Her hair was dark, untamed and short, stopping just at her chin. Her eyes were wide and tired and blue, and her expression was one of bewilderment.

She touched her face, feeling the smooth texture of her skin, the feel of her hair, the light scar on her cheek, standing out against her darker tone.

The scar.

Madison leaned in closer to the water, trying to get a better look at it.

It was faint, barely noticeable, but definitely there. Madison frowned, remembering the gentle hands that had patched it up for her. She held a hand to it for a moment, staring through her reflection into the depths of the lake.

She frowned even more when she realised that the scar was just more proof that her dreams were actually memories.

"What's wrong?" Jason's voice came from behind as he sat down beside her.

He saw her staring intently at her reflection in the

water, saw the distressed look on her face and put two and two together.

Or so he thought.

"Don't worry. You don't look that bad. Besides, it doesn't matter what you look like here anyway-"

He was silenced with a splash of cold water to his face.

As he coughed and spluttered, she smirked widely. For such a smart boy, he could be really stupid sometimes.

"That's not what I was frowning at, you."

She stood up. Her smirk had evolved into a wide grin.

Jason got up too, wiping water from his eyes. He stared at her, accepting an imaginary challenge. Then his eyes locked onto something behind her and his expression turned into one of fear.

Without even thinking, Madison whipped around at lightning speed, searching around for danger of any kind.

What she hadn't been expecting was a blast of cool water from behind.

Madison stood there, soaked, while Jason cackled madly at his ingenious plan.

"Why you..." she muttered quietly. She sighed, knowing that she would be unable to let this slide. He had gotten her hoodie wet.

That was something she couldn't forgive.

She unzipped her hoodie, laying it carefully on the ground. Next she rolled up the sleeves of the white shirt she wore underneath and her leggings, right up to her knees.

Jason faltered, knowing she was up to something. Was she mad at him? Maybe he shouldn't have gotten her hoodie wet. He knew how much she liked it-

He wasn't given any time to breath as Madison flashed towards him at the speed of light, grabbing him by the waist. Jason soon realised where they were headed.

"No. No, please! I'm sorry-"

It was too late.

The two of them plunged into the lake. Although the day was so hot, the water was freezing. While Jason was coming to terms with the cold, Madison showed no mercy, dousing him in splash after splash of water. Jason soon got up, and began to retaliate.

The whole world was quiet, apart from the waterfall, the splashes of water, and their laughter. For once in Madison's life, everything was perfect. She wished it could stay this way forever, just her and Jason, in this wonderful place.

Then the boy from her memory flashed in her mind, and she felt unexplainably guilty.

Eventually, they got tired, their splashes becoming energy deprived and effortless.

They lay down, their backs on the warm grass, drying themselves in the sun.

Madison knew fully well that this was all just a distraction from the real task at hand.

Finding the Source.

Even though she had no clue what the Source actually was, she knew it was important, judging by its name.

But then the question came up in her mind.

Did they really have to find it?

Couldn't she and Jason just stay here, untroubled by the world around them, living in their own paradise?

Even thinking it didn't seem right. Madison didn't like

the idea of sitting around, when there was something she needed to do.

She very much doubted that her old life tolerated much sitting around, anyway.

The creature they had seen before took over her thoughts, the very memory filling her insides with fear.

She got up quickly.

"Where are you off to?" Jason's large green eyes stared up at her. He looked troubled, like she had just snapped him out of a dream.

 Or a nightmare.

"Just getting some more fruit. You want some?"

It wasn't exactly a lie. She had been thinking about getting more of those delicious fruit.

Jason shook his head, and Madison took off.

Nearer to the waterfall, the crashing of the water got louder, loud enough to drown Madison's thoughts.

That was good. She needed that.

The trees which bore the fruit were right next to the waterfall, and the crashing was deafening there.

She didn't mind.

True to her word, she picked one of the fruit from the tree. As she took a bite, she began to feel better. Memories of the mist creature and the talking wolf already felt more distant.

At the corner of her eye, she noticed a dark gap between the cascading water, and the bed of rock of the waterfall. Even more than that, there was a strange glow coming from it. It was very faint, but quite evident. She squinted her eyes, making sure she wasn't hallucinating or something. The light was still there.

She was filled with an unexplained curiosity. Something told her that she had to find out what it was. Dropping the fruit from her hand, she made her way towards the gap in the waterfall, as though in a trance.

Suddenly, all that mattered was finding out what that glow was.

Madison slipped through the gap, the spray from the waterfall spattering her newly dried clothes. She heard her name being called from outside, but she ignored it. The voice was so far away.

And insignificant.

The cave she had found was dark, but the glow was brighter than it had been before.

She just had to locate it.

Feeling her way through the darkness, she slowly made her way through the cave. In the large space, even the slight sound of her feet on the ground was amplified.

The light got brighter and brighter, and soon she didn't need to grasp the wall for support, she could see perfectly fine on her own.

"Madison!" she heard someone call her name, close to the entrance.

She paid no heed.

As she got closer, she noticed tiny specks of dust floating through the air.

But they weren't regular specks of dust.

They were bright blue.

And glowing.

This only heightened Madison's resolve to get to the bright light.

She accelerated her speed from a walk, to a jog, to a run,

feeling impatient yet patient, unprepared but ready all at the same time.

All the while, the concentration of glowing dust in the air seemed to increase the closer she got to her destination.

She turned a corner, and was hit with the brightest, bluest light she had ever experienced.

When her eyes adjusted, she couldn't believe what she was looking at.

A vast array of bright blue flowers connected by ivy grew from every orifice they could find, exuding the purest blue light she had ever seen. They were everywhere, twisted around stalactites, stalagmites and pillars, entwining themselves while spreading on the walls and even on the roof of the cave.

All the flowers seemed to grow back to one spot at the edge of the cave.

That spot gave off the most glow out of everything there.

Madison had never felt surer of anything in her life then the fact that she had to get to that glowing light.

She tried to identify what it was that she was feeling at that moment, but her mind came up blank.

All she could come up with was a definite sureness.

And a strange yearning in the pit of her stomach.

She made her way slowly across the illuminated chamber, staring at all the flowers she passed.

She crouched down and picked one that was clinging on a stalagmite.

It disintegrated into blue dust at her touch, diffusing into the air and going separate ways.

Madison stopped, watching the particles disperse, feeling strangely calm. She shouldn't be.

She'd just found a secret cave full of glowing flowers, and she'd left Jason alone without saying anything. Jason would be so worried. He'd-

Any thoughts of Jason disappeared as a strong force tugged at Madison's gut. She was drawn to the direction of the light.

It seemed to beckon her, call her.

She rose to her feet.

Everything else was cleared from her mind. She knew her goal.

She knew her purpose.

"Madison!" Jason's resurfaced, closer than before. She didn't even look back.

She realised now. He was just a hindrance to her. To what she had to do.

She walked towards the light.

"No! Don't go there! It's dangerous!"

Dangerous? She scoffed silently. The only dangerous thing here would be her if he kept on getting in her way.

It was so close now. Just a few steps away.

Three more steps.

Two more steps.

One more step.

A hand reached for hers and yanked her back. She stumbled, nearly falling to the ground.

She shook with anger as the hindrance walked in front of her.

Blocking her view of the light.

"I can't let you go there. I meant it when I said it was

dangerous. Let's go back now."

Go back?! After coming all this way?

Her anger suddenly rose to its peak.

Don't hold back, don't hold back, don't hold back-

She didn't hold back.

The blue light got brighter, brighter, until it was all she could see.

"Get out of my way!"

She pushed the hindrance out of the way, making towards the light.

Everything would be fine as long as she got to it.

The hindrance grabbed her leg, making her trip and fall yet again.

Before she could right herself again, he seized her wrists and dragged her away.

Away from the light.

Away from her power.

Away from her freedom.

She lost it. She kicked and screamed and bit wherever she could, flailing in all directions.

The hindrance just held on tighter, doing everything in his power to get her away from that light.

The struggling match went on for a few more minutes, until she got too tired to keep up with him.

"Madison, snap out of it. Whatever this is, we'll figure it out, but right now, I need you to let me help you. Please."

She didn't want to listen to a single word of what he said, so she kept kicking and flailing, desperate to get out of his grasp.

"If you really wanted to help me, you'd let me go!" she growled, not slowing down.

What she hadn't expected was for him to actually let her go.

She looked at his face.

Everything stopped.

It was as if she was being snapped out of a terrible nightmare, one of the kind that felt dreadfully real, that made you wake up drenched in sweat, yet shivering in fear.

Jason was crying, tears leaking from his worn, tired eyes.

"Please," he whispered again, "I don't want to hurt you."

And that's when the horror of what she'd done crashed over her, the heavy weight of shame settling over her shoulders.

She'd hurt the person she'd sworn to protect.

And that was worse than anything else that could have happened.

"What have I done?" she murmured fearfully, looking up at Jason.

He said nothing, but pulled her into a tight hug.

"It wasn't your fault" he whispered, tears still streaming down his face.

All the laughter from earlier was gone, replaced with a heavy, burdened silence, weighing on Madison's shoulders more than ever before.

She knew Jason was just trying to make her feel better. She appreciated it.

But she knew in her heart that it was her fault.

Everything was her fault.

Monster, the children from her memory echoed in her

mind.

She understood where they were coming from now.

CHAPTER 7

THE TWO OF THEM DECIDED TO GET AS FAR AWAY FROM THE CAVE AS
POSSIBLE, as neither wanted a repeat of their recent
experience.

A sombre mood settled over the two as they grabbed
some fruit to bring back to the shore with them, neither
uttering a word. Madison picked up her hoodie from
where she left it on the ground, and took one last look
around before they left.

She glanced at the waterfall, but turned away quickly as
the memory of the glowing cave came back to her.

She never wanted to admit this to Jason, but she still felt
inexplicably drawn to that cave.

It had taken all her strength to walk away from it, and
being in close proximity to it wasn't helping.

A silent agreement was reached between them that it

was time for them to leave.

Madison turned on her heels in a flash, eager to leave this all behind her.

Although it was nice to be back underneath the familiar canopy of trees, she couldn't relax. Experience had reminded her again and again over these past two days that she would never be safe on this island.

The ever persistent talking wolf (she still had a hard time processing that) could appear again at any time, but she wouldn't have the strength to defend or attack, given the state she was in.

She didn't even want to touch the other possibility.

The monster whose stare was like the definition of fear.

Madison still didn't understand how Jason escaped it unscathed.

Or did he? She had never thought to ask him.

She turned her head over to him to do so, but stopped immediately.

His face was twisted into an awful grimace, eyes blurry and fixated ahead of him. It was clear for anyone to see that he was distressed about something, but unwilling to talk about it.

Another wave of guilt rushed over her as she considered herself as being the cause of his unease.

She sighed in frustration. Nothing was going well for them, and what was meant to be relaxing and fun had turned into yet another thing to be confused and scared about.

Frustration built up inside her.

Why did they have to be scared of the things they were ignorant about?

The best thing would be to find out about them, building up knowledge until they weren't a threat anymore. Nobody was going to give them any answers, or do anything for them. So in a heartbeat, Madison decided to do what felt natural to her, what she had probably been doing her whole life anyway.

She'd do it herself.

"I've had enough of this" Jason spoke up. Madison snapped her head towards him, not expecting him to talk.

"Enough of what?"

"Enough of *this*" he gestured all around him, at the entire forest.

Madison raised an eyebrow.

"You'll have to be more specific than that."

Jason shot her a glare, and Madison, reminded of the incident not up to half an hour ago, looked away.

"You know exactly what I mean. I'm tired of being here, with no idea how or why. I'm sick of not knowing anything. Of not *understanding* anything. If I'm going to stay here, I'm going to need some answers."

They look at each other, and see the same ambition in each others' eyes.

They had both been thinking about the same thing.

"We're the only ones we can rely on. Nobody can just give us the answers."

Madison nodded, fixing her gaze on the tall trees ahead of her.

"If we put together everything that we know right now, we can get some sort of understanding of our situation in general. But where do we start?"

She thought she had a point. The numbers of things

they didn't know greatly outweighed the things that they did know, and even with their limited knowledge, their information was incomplete and jumbled in various places.

"We start from the beginning of our memories. From there, we figure out what we can from each memory, and piece it all together to get a general idea of what's going on. It's not as efficient as it could be, but we haven't exactly been left with many options."

"Sounds fine to me. Let's start from the first memory we got." Jason nodded in reply.

Madison began to recount what had happened in the memory, adding in any slight detail which may have been of importance. As she talked, the sombre mood from earlier lightened into something more curious and riveting.

At the end of her account, Jason confirmed that he had the same memory, apart from the different view perspective.

"What could we learn from that, though? Nothing really stands out to me" Madison asked, her forehead wrinkling as she thought.

Jason thought to himself before answering.

"Well, we know that the memory wasn't recent. We were younger, maybe seven or eight."

"Oh yeah. I forgot about that."

"And we also know that the place we were at was where we lived. Do you remember anything else about it?"

Madison shook her head.

"Alright. I don't think there was anything else

important to our situation in that. What about the next memory?"

"The one with that 'Master' guy in it. I'm still trying to wrap my head around the whole thing."

Jason scoffed lightly.

"Anything new about that? Anyway, there were quite a few notable events in that memory that might be of use to us now."

"Like what?"

"The first thing is the fact that you were trying to escape. I remember you said something about being treated differently from the other kids. That means we lived with other people, and the reason they didn't like us was probably because of our powers."

"So basically what you're saying is that we lived with a bunch of morons who hated our guts because we were different?"

"Putting it a little... strongly, yes. But that's not the only thing that we could take from this memory. We know that you were able to use your powers. I'm not sure exactly what it was, but it seemed like you were able to-"

"Create glowing dust out of thin air? Yeah, so cool. Definitely cooler than being able to split the crust of the earth by merely stomping your foot, or creating giant holes in the earth so deep and dark, they seem endless. Very useful, too. You never know when the beach will run out of sand."

Jason shook his head woefully.

"Madison, I don't believe comparing our powers will do us any good. And besides, yours could be more than you think."

"Oh really?"

"Yes really. Have you ever wondered where all that dust comes from?"

Madison opened her mouth to supply an answer, but her mind came up blank. Jason actually had a point, as usual.

Seeing that she couldn't come up with an answer, Jason gave her a victorious grin.

"See? Not everything has to be black and white. There's always going to be more than one side to things."

Madison rolled her eyes, seeing the triumphant look on his face.

"Yeah, yeah. Lesson learnt. Now what about the thing we were talking about before?"

"The important events? The most obvious and important one would be about the Master."

"Well, what exactly about him? Apart from the fact that he's an egotistical old man who is somehow the mysterious driving force behind all the bad things going on in my life."

Jason gave her a look that seemed to radiate pure confusion.

"What did he ever do to you!? From my recollection, he helped us escape from certain punishment, *and* offered us to train with him to enhance and control our powers."

"And from *my* recollection, Jason, people don't normally do things for you without an ulterior motive. Take you for example. In the first memory, why did you stay with me in the corridor? And don't try and say "It was the right thing to do" because I know that's not the truth."

Jason stared at the forest floor, eyes narrowed in thought.

" But it *is* the truth. You were my friend, and I didn't want you to be alone. And, I guess it's because I was curious as well. I wanted to know what happened earlier on to get you in that state. But it was out of worry, of course" he replied.

"Even so, it proves my point. You weren't doing it completely from the bottom of your heart. You wanted information from me."

"And to be with my friend?" Jason offered weakly.

"We're alone on a deserted island with only a few memories of our old lives. At least you got what you wanted."

"And now I'm beginning to regret it."

"But just imagine this. If you did such a little favour like keeping me company and expected a small thing in return, like information, the Master must be expecting something huge from us."

"Sure, but we don't know that yet."

"It's not a matter of 'if.' It's 'what.'"

"Well, whatever it is that's going on with him, he definitely has something to do with us being here."

Jason paused to step over a fallen log, Madison doing the same.

"The last part of the dream was different. The memory had changed to a different time. Something big had just happened, but I can't remember what."

Madison inhaled sharply, remembering the horrible feeling of hopelessness that had ensnared her, of loss and fear.

"We did something bad."

Jason stopped, and stared.

"What?"

"We did something bad, unforgivable, but I can't remember what. But at the same time, I kind of don't want to know. During it, I heard the Master's voice."

"Really? I didn't hear anything. What did he say?"

Madison took in a shaky inhaled breath.

"He told me to find the Source."

Madison waited for Jason to respond, to say anything, but he didn't open his mouth for a good few minutes. She looked in his direction, and understood why.

He had 'the face.'

He knew something.

"What is it?" she asked, lowering her voice for some reason.

Jason stared straight ahead, taking in a deep gulp.

"In the cave. Why were you the only one who got affected by that light?"

She looked at him, surprised.

"I don't know. It was like…the light was calling me. To come back to it. As if we were one."

Jason frowned.

"So you were right after all."

"What do you mean? I'm never right."

Jason brought his gaze back to her, seriousness hardening his eyes.

"About the Master. There's way more to him than we thought. And there's a reason why he chose us to be his students."

"Could you please explain? Not all of us speak code."

"But I wasn't- never mind. What I'm saying is, I think the light in that cave, is the Source."

There was silence again, but this time Jason waited for Madison to speak.

"Why do you think he chose us to be his students?" she asked in a deathly quiet voice.

"This is just an guess considering what you told me, but since you're the only one that reacted to the Source, you might be the only one that can… use whatever the Source is used for. It's just a guess. I'm not sure why he chose me, though."

When he finished talking, there was no response.

"What? You have nothing to say?"

Madison stayed silent.

"We have to go back."

Madison spontaneously grabbed him by the hand, gripping tightly.

"No, we don't" she replied, deathly serious. "We can't ever go back there again. I won't ever."

Jason jumped, startled by her reaction.

"Why not? The Source is probably the only reason we're on this island. If we bring it back, this could all be over!"

"We don't know that!"

"Well, it's the only lead we have. Why are you so reluctant!?"

They were standing face to face, inches away from each other. Madison dropped her gaze to the floor, her energy draining away.

"Seeing you hurt and scared was a terrible thing. What was even worse was the fact that I had caused it, and I don't want to see that happen again."

Hearing this, Jason's face softened, and a sad smile appeared on his lips.

"You don't have to worry about me. I'd be fine, since I know what to expect next time. You should worry more about yourself. You don't know what would happen if you went to the light."

"But what about after? What if I'm not the same? What if that feeling I had when I went to the light comes back and I'm not able to-"

"That's enough." Jason said sternly. "Don't you remember what you told me yesterday? If you loose your head, you'll never see the end of this. Don't tell me you only said that to shut me up."

Madison looked at him, smiling slightly.

"Maybe that was part of it."

Jason shook his head exasperatedly, taking some of the fruit from earlier out of his pocket.

"Take it. When we get back to the shore, we'll rest for a bit. Then we'll come back to find the Source."

Madison took the fruit from him, taking a bite and loosing herself in the taste that she had come to love.

Thinking about it, she found that they had a pretty good lead. Jason was right. Once they found the Source, they could have a way of finally getting off this island. Then all they had to do was find the Master and get him to spill his guts about what was going on.

But some gut feeling told her that it wouldn't be that easy. Nothing ever was.

She found her mind wandering back to earlier events. The wolf. Why did he want the Source? And why did he think she had it? They had the big picture, but they didn't have all the little details. It was frustrating.

And the creature…

"Jason?" Madison asked before she was even aware of it.

"Yeah?"

"The creature from earlier…what happened to it? Did it do anything to you? How did you escape?"

The hunching of Jason's shoulders didn't go unnoticed to her.

"It just… went away" he replied without looking at her.

Madison could tell that he wasn't telling the truth.

But at the same time, he wasn't exactly lying to her.

She wanted the entire truth.

There were too many things she only had half the information for, and she didn't need to higher the number.

"What exactly happened after I passed out? Did it do something to you?"

Jason stayed quiet.

"Did you… do something to it?"

"That's enough! I'll tell you when I want to tell you, and I don't want to right now."

"But if it's still wandering around, we need to be prepared for it!"

"Trust me. It's gone."

Jason's tone was final and absolute as he abruptly ended the conversation before it could turn heated.

Madison sighed and continued the long journey back to the shore.

Something told her that just because they knew a bit

more than they initially did didn't mean that things would get any easier for them.

Part 2

Alone

CHAPTER 8

THE BAR WAS HOT AND CROWDED AS THE MASTER TOOK HIS PLACE
AT A ROUND TABLE IN A SHADED CORNER.

Despite being shabby and rundown, it was always full
whenever he came by.

His shoes scuffed the dirty wooden floorboards, and he
found his eyes wandering over to the wallpaper, which
was worn down from age and layer upon layer of scum.
None of the people here seemed to care about the bar's
unattractive interior.

It's not the view they came for.

He knew it was rude to stare, but he always found it
interesting to watch the people who came and went.

Most ambled in with their heads hung low, eyes dead

and staring, not a shred of hope visible.

And most staggered out into the permanently dark night singing drunken songs, laughing about nothing. Full of newfound hope.

It was almost like magic.

He checked his watch impatiently.

It wasn't like them to be late.

Just as he thought that, the door opened once again, his two oldest students stepping into the bar.

A few even stopped their incessant drinking to look at them.

They weren't overdressed, loud or boisterous. Each had an air of authority, demanding respect from all who looked.

Just as he taught them.

The woman had the same serious gaze as always, eyes unblinking as she scanned the room thoughtfully. Dark curly hair was combed back into a neat bun at her nape. Her complexion was dark, her stare deadpan.

The man hadn't changed a bit, cerulean eyes darting around curiously. A peak of white hair spilled out from under his navy beanie, a shocking contrast.

They spotted him in his corner of the room and made their way over.

"You're really here."

The Master looked at them, taking in their presence, smiling. They'd grown so much, barely looked like the children he'd trained.

"Marinique and Alder. It's been a while. How've you been keeping?"

The woman gave a loud huff.

"I go by Maria these days. It's less suspicious if I use a regular name. And we were keeping well, until you called us out of the blue when we thought you were gone for good. Next time you disappear off the face of the earth, make sure you do it permanently."

The Master let out a laugh, Alder doing the same.

"That was years ago" Alder said.

"Exactly my point" she replied coldly.

They proceeded to assume two empty chairs on opposite sides of the table.

"How's your research going, Alder? Any headway yet?"

"It's off to a rocky start, but most researches usually begin like that. The dark mist present in the atmosphere has been going up steadily for a few days now. It's going to take a while to figure out why, and how to decrease it. But what have you been getting up to all this time?"

The Master gave a small smile.

"It's complicated."

Maria sighed in her chair impatiently.

"So what matter of such urgency is there that you decided to come back into existence?" she asked, sarcasm evident in her tone.

"I'm glad you asked. I have a favour to ask you both."

The two went silent, waiting for the Master to continue.

"You remember I've been looking for the Sources, don't you?"

At the mention of it, the two gave each other a glance.

"Have you found one?" Maria questioned.

"No. But I've found people who will."

"Would you mind filling us in, then? They're especially hard to find. And even if these people did find one, they'd have to be a trained vessel to use it."

"So who are they? Are they trained? And experienced?"

The Master sighed.

"No and no. I found two eligible people for the job a few years ago. I trained them myself in order for them to carry out this task. A girl and a boy."

Maria's eye twitched.

"Wait. You mean… children? You picked children to do this job for you?! You've done some questionable things in your past, but this is by far the most senile!"

"Why did you chose them?"

The Master shook his head.

"These two would definitely be able to handle the task. The girl's one of the toughest people I know, and the boy's so smart he could put any of us adults to shame. Believe me, this wasn't some whimsical decision."

"I'll take your word for it. They're smart and tough, but how does that make them any different from all the other people who've tried to find it?"

The Master placed his elbows on the table, holding his hands up to his face.

"Another important factor would be that they're Source vessels."

Maria made a weird strangled sound.

"You could have said that earlier!" she hissed through her teeth.

"How on earth did you manage to find *two* Source vessels? And in the same place?"

"Luck. It comes to me naturally."

"And you said they're trained? So they'll be able to take the power?"

"Not exactly. They're still kids, so the power would be too much for them to control."

There was a long pause before he continued.

"That's why I had to erase their memories."

"You what!?" both Alder and Maria shouted simultaneously.

This time they caught a few strange stares in their direction from other tables.

"Great. Now they're paying attention to us." Maria muttered, glaring daggers at the Master.

He raised his hands up in defence.

"I didn't do anything!"

"Are you three ordering anything?"

The bartender watched them sourly.

She was short and skinny, her feet tapping on the floor

impatiently. Her mousy hair was limp and ragged, her white jumper full of stains, unwashed.

"You can't just sit there without getting something."

"I'll have a beer, please" Alder said loudly.

"Same here" Maria followed.

"And what about you, sir?" the bartender asked the Master, eyeing him curiously.

"I'll have some apple juice."

This earned him three weird stares.

"Uh…alright. Right away" the bartender hobbled off.

Two pairs of eyes snapped back to the Master when he was gone.

"You have a lot of explaining to do" Maria stated.

He sighed, sitting up in his chair.

"About what? Why I erased their memories, or why I chose to drink apple juice at a bar?"

Maria's eyes narrowed.

"I can't believe I forgot how annoying you are."

The Master straightened up, serious now.

"I did it for two main reasons. If they remembered how to use their powers and what I taught them on top of finding the Source, the power would be too much for one to handle. I made it so that parts of their memories would come back to them every time they go to sleep. I know they'll remember what they're on the island to do. The second reason was the fact that they might not want to come back. They lived in the confinement building when I found them. In fact, they were trying to run away the first time we met. If they were given the choice to come back to a dark world where few cared about them, or stay in an isolated place where nobody could bother them, there's a possibility where they might not return."

That's not the real reason why he did it. He knew if they remembered what they had done before they left, they simply wouldn't have been able to carry out the task.

"What if they're not able to find the Source?" Alder asked.

"I wouldn't worry about that, Alder. I know they'll find it. They're stubborn kids, the pair of them."

It was their stubbornness that got us into this mess to begin with.

"Then if everything's going smoothly, why did you call us here? Is something not going to plan?"

"Everything's going to plan. For now. I need to ask you both a favour."

Alder and Maria exchanged glances.

"We're listening."

The bartender returned with their drinks.

"Here" she said, handing each their own mug.

The Master took a sip of his juice. The flavour was weak and unappetising. But he wasn't going to complain. Luxury was something that very few could afford in this world anymore.

"Thanks" he smiled. The woman watched him, her eyes

lingering for a minute longer than they should have. She promptly left .

"Well? Are you going to tell us what it is?" Alder asked, impatient.

The Master took another swig of his juice before answering.

"I need one of you to take the Source vessel in."

He was met with silence.

"You said there were two. What will happen to the other?"

"There are… some issues he needs to work out."

Issues was an understatement.

"What kind of issues?"

The city- destroying kind.

"Nothing really. Just a few things he has to work out about his powers."

He raised his glass.

"There's another problem. I think the P.E.C have caught wind of the Source's location."

Alder's expression darkened.

"What would they want with the Source?"

"What else would they want it for? Testing its properties, experiments. Power transferals. Do the kids know about them?"

"I'd say not. They must have figured out the Source's location. Maybe they've already encountered one of them. Their artificial powers would allow them to be elusive."

"How do you expect them to defend themselves?" Maria asked.

"I said that I erased their memories, but I didn't erase their powers. It's a part of them, so they'll find a way to use them eventually."

"I don't like this at all."

"And you don't have to. All you need to do is help them."

"To really help them would be to keep them out of our matters completely!"

"I would be unable to keep them out of things. Especially since they were the ones who brought up the amounts of dark mist in the atmosphere in the first place."

Alder choked on his drink.

Maria's face seemed to be frozen in a permanently horrified position, her mouth gaping.

"They...what?" Alder spluttered.

"Just who are these kids? How did they manage to do something like that?"

"Good question. And you know what will happen if the amount goes up any further."

A silence followed, each considering the deadly consequences.

"Which Source have you found?" Alder quietly asked.

"The Source of creation."

He nodded slowly.

"And...if we find it, and the vessel is able to take the

power, we might be able to lower it?"

"I can't say for sure. But it's the only thing that we have for now."

He gave them both a serious look.

"This is where the both of you come in. I need one of you to take the Source vessel in. What you would need to do is to look after her, train her, get her to use her powers properly. And after that, I'll tell you the rest."

Maria and Alder gave each other a look.

"I can't take the kid in. I have too much going on, and a lab isn't exactly a safe place for a child" Alder remarked, putting his hands up.

"I could do it. I've got some property here in the north where we could stay. Though it does need a bit of redecorating. I haven't been there in years. And I figure there are a few things I could teach her as well."

The Master gave her a wide smile.

"Perfect. Now, that leaves you, Alder."

Alder looked at the Master curiously.

He pulled out a small satchel from under the table, and the two stared at it, scepticism prominent in their expressions. He opened it reverently, taking out a small blade.

It was nothing out of the ordinary, apart from the small glinting red crystal at the hilt.

"I need you to take this somewhere… important. Make sure you treat this with care, because trust me, this is no ordinary blade. I'll need you to get it there as soon as possible."

"Where exactly am I taking it?"

The Master leaned in closer at the table, whispering the words carefully.

He got his intended reaction.

Maria gaped at him.

Alder's expression darkened.

"You expect me to do anything for those traitors?" he hissed.

"They're not traitors. They were just doing what they thought was right."

"Well, your vision of right would have to be extremely wrong if you're going to think that what they did was okay."

"I never supported it. I still don't."

"I'm not going there. I'm never stepping foot into that treacherous city."

The Master sighed, taking a small sip of his drink.

"That's too bad, considering that I called you here to help us. Even after everything I've done for you..."

Alder sighed, not looking happy at all.

"You guilt tripper. Fine. I'll do it. But what do I do when I get there? Do I give it to them face to face and deliver the message? Or do I just prop it there with a note?"

"You decide however you want to do it. Though it

would be preferable if you gave it to them face to face. It would alarm them to the urgency of the situation."

He leaned in closer.

"Though I must warn you. It will be harder to get in than before. The barrier gets stronger with each passing day since the acceleration. And very soon it will be impermeable to even the most skilled of us."

Alder looked away thoughtfully.

"I'll have to get going soon, then."

The Master nodded, fishing something out from his pocket.

"Here's what you have to tell them" he said, handing him a folded piece of paper. Alder took it, opening it immediately. He scanned through it once.

And again.

And a third time.

His eyes were wider and his expression more alarmed.

"So that's…" his eyes moved towards the blade.

"Let me see" Maria demanded, snatching it off him.

Her reaction was similar to Alder's as she read the note.

"You can't be serious. Where did you find that?" she whispered.

"Another story that I have neither the time or will to tell. Well, now you know. Alder, can you give me your word that this will be delivered to the city as soon as possible?" the Master asked, expression stern.

Alder folded the paper carefully, putting it in his pocket.

"Of course" he answered quietly.

"I have a question" Maria stated.

"I'm all ears."

"What will you be doing during all of this? I think you should be the one to take the kid. You owe them a proper explanation as to what's going on. I wouldn't be able to give a sufficient amount. And this will be hard on the vessel. I'm a stranger who they've never seen in their life, who has to look after them."

The Master set down his drink.

"I have to go somewhere. There's something important I need to do as well. And as for the other part, it can be solved with a simple note. I can give one to you to show her when she gets there."

Maria nodded, arms folded.

"I think that's all I wanted to tell you about."

Alder leaned back in his chair.

"I can't believe this. One moment, I'm living my relatively normal life, and the next, the Master returns and summons me to a life- changing secret meeting in which he informs me of the vessels of the Source. And now I have to go to the place I hate most in the world-"

"A place you've never been to before" Maria interrupted.

"Don't you know what they did? Why wouldn't I hate everything about them? A city built on a foundation of lies and betrayal?" Alder asked.

Maria sighed, raising a glass to her lips. She regarded the Master.

"Seriously though. This is so out of the blue. I can't even remember the last time I saw you. But I guess that's just the life of a Master, huh?"

The Master himself let out a loud sigh, taking a swig from his apple juice.

"You have no idea. I never get a free minute! And I've been busier than ever, these days."

Maria put her arms on the desk, locking her hands together in front of her face.

"Doing what exactly?" she asked suspiciously.

"It's confidential, my friend. Nothing's coming out of these lips."

Maria scowled menacingly at him, while Alder stifled his laugh.

"But seriously, though. I'm worried about these kids. Do they know anything about the P.E.C?"

"Unfortunately not. Perhaps they've encountered them more than once by now. It wouldn't be as obvious. They've found all sorts of ways to replicate the Particles present in people who can use powers. So now they're able to use artificial powers. I'm sure they'll be very discrete about it as well."

Maria looked down to her lap, a frown developing on her face.

"What're their names?"

"Madison and Jason. The Source vessel is Madison."

"Those don't sound like transcender names" Alder noted absent- mindedly.

"Then why is Jason on the island? If Madison is the one who needs to find the Source, why's he there?"

"Contact with a person from your past is what triggers the memories. And besides, those two bring out the best in each other."

Raucous laughter sounded from the table near them, the inhabitants bursting out into drunken song. Soon the whole bar had joined in.

The only reason he had decided to have the meeting in this bar was because they could easily blend in with the hoards of people. There was nothing better than hiding in plain sight.

Transcenders weren't exactly tolerated after what happened all those years ago.

Alder stood up, buttoning up his coat. His mug was still relatively full on the table.

"If that's all you have to say, I'd better get going. I have some business to attend to. And the noise here is becoming too much to handle."

"We'll come with you. It is getting noisy in here." the Master replied.

They got up, scooting around several round tables to get to the door opposite the bar stand.

The stare of the bartender as they passed didn't go

unnoticed to the Master.

Maria opened the door, letting in a large gust of freezing wind. She shivered.

"I haven't been here for ages. I've forgotten how bad it is."

"You think here is bad? Antartica has become uninhabitable" Alder said.

The Master blinked a few times. It would've been completely dark if a few street lamps didn't light the way, spattering weak light on their surroundings.

They exited the bar.

He didn't ignore the figure lurking behind a lamppost not too far away from them.

"Hey there! Leaving already?" a slurred and overly friendly voice boomed. Alder turned around to find a large man with a round shiny head grinning at him.

He looked calm and unperturbed as he replied.

"Yes I am. I've had enough drinks for one day."

"Well, unfortunately, we can't let you leave. The bartender told us to keep an eye on you."

Maria let out an exasperated sigh.

"I knew there was something fishy about that lady."

"I thought it was kind of obvious. That was the worst apple juice I'd ever tasted in my life."

The bald man gave them a smirk, and let out a loud bellow.

"They're tryn'a leave, m'am!" he hollered.

The bartender appeared at the door.

"What exactly have we done wrong?" The Master asked.

The bartender stared him in the eye, a bitter smile on her lips, strands of straggly hair falling down her face.

"Well sir, I hope you realise what a versatile question it is that you've asked me. But if you're looking for a straight answer…"

She took a step closer, the smile vanishing, showcasing her menacing exterior.

"You're transcenders-"

A small group of three other people formed around them, none looking too happy-

"And you have the nerve to walk into my bar as if you have the *right.*"

Alder raised his eyebrows, as if he had heard this all before.

"We're humans too. Unfortunately, people like you don't seem to realise that."

The bartender's expression turned to one of anger.

"You know, the P.E.C pay really well for transcenders. We could just report you, and they'll come running. Experiments are all you people are good for. So, its either you turn yourself in willingly, or you've got a fight on your hands. Your odds don't look very good for the latter, by the way."

Alder and Maria spared a glance at each other, and then

the Master.

"Should I make it quick?" Maria asked.

The Master sighed, stifling a yawn.

"Alright. I'm too tired, anyway. Try not to make too much noise."

They turned to the small group.

The Master could see a pale golden light rise from Maria's palm, which she hid behind her back.

"Who told you about us?" Alder asked.

The bartender scoffed.

"Do you really think I'd give *you* information? Let's just get this over with-"

She was promptly silenced when Maria drew her hand out, the pale shine becoming a golden glow.

She snapped her fingers, the small sound resonating in the darkness.

Each person in the small group gave an unexpected jolt.

They began to look around confusedly, unaware of why they were standing there.

"Huh. Guess I'll go back inside" the bartender muttered, doing just that.

The others looked around in a daze, following suit.

"I taught you both well" the Master stated, stroking his moustache in approval.

Maria frowned.

"It took longer to set in than usual."

"Ah well. We're getting old. It must be that."

"Nonsense! I'm older than both of you, and I haven't lost my touch" the Master corrected.

"You don't count as a valid example for anything. You're a Master, which means you have to be good at everything, for some reason."

"That's not true. I've never been able to get the hang of volleyball."

"That's enough, you two. Nobody was supposed to know about us. So why did that just happen?" Maria asked.

The Master's eyes flew to the person watching them from the streetlamp.

"I can only think of one explanation."

Without warning, he lit his hand with a ball of golden light, sending it at full blast. As he expected, the person vanished, not a trace of their presence left behind.

"Who the hell was that?! Did he just disappear?"

"No. He disassembled his Particles. It seems we have a stalker."

"From where?"

Maria's eyes hardened.

"The P.E.C, of course. They know about us now."

"Not good" Alder remarked.

"Now that they know that we're involved with the Source, our job will get a lot harder."

The Master stared out into the pitch black sky.

The sight was no different from closing his eyes.

He thought of the two children he had sent out to a strange new place.

"And so will theirs."

Chapter 9

The sky was so strange.

It was never the same whenever Madison looked up.

Some times, it was clear and blue, not a hint of any other colour or texture in it. Other times, there were tinges of pink and orange, streaks of purple, splashes of colours unfamiliar and strange.

She liked it, but it still puzzled her.

Why did it have to change all the time? Couldn't it just stay one way and be like that forever?

And why did gazing at it feel so new to her?

She looked up and saw the stars. They illuminated the darkness and all her fears and worries crumbled away.

They always had that effect on her. Staring at them reminded her of something, unreachable yet tangible.

Something hopeful.

She liked the sky better at this time. No matter what it looked like during the day, she could always count on the same sight at night.

How long has it been now since she's seen them?

Something told her it's been a long time.

Or maybe she never did.

She brought her eyes down to the fire she was sitting in front of.

The flames looked like they were dancing, a beautiful, ethereal dance that no other substance could replicate. Fire was like magic. Wasn't it magic? It was created seemingly in the same way that magic was.

From nothing.

But there was one difference between the two.

Fire has an explanation.

Magic doesn't.

Is that why the people from her memory didn't like her? Because she couldn't be explained?

What if they were right? Right that her powers were bad, and ultimately made her a worse person?

Maybe that's why she attacked Jason earlier on when she tried to get to the Source.

"Deep in thought?" Jason asked, sitting down beside her. Madison sighed.

"Don't even get me started."

Neither of them said anything more. A comfortable silence was reached as they both brought their gazes to the mystery filled sky, revelling in the peace of a night that was theirs. Madison closed her eyes.

She didn't want to have to think. Just for now. Maybe if she stayed still for a long enough time, she could make it happen. She wouldn't have to worry about any of the memories plaguing her mind. She wouldn't have to focus on her anger, or hatred.

Or the compromising fear in her that she refused to acknowledge.

She turned to Jason, who was lying in the long grass.

"What're you thinking about?" she asked.

"That's not a question I could answer quickly, you know. There's too much."

"Yeah, I know. But tell me anyway. I need a distraction. And I want to know."

Jason closed his eyes, thinking for a minute.

"I'll make a list. I'm thinking about my memories, the time I've spent here, the things that happened. I'm trying to figure out answers. And, I'm thinking about the Source, and you. I'm wondering what connection you have to it. And when you said that we did something bad, I still don't remember what that was. And- well, you get the point."

Madison nodded.

"Yes. Yes I do."

She lay down beside him, and lifted his chin up to the sky.

To the stars.

"What we need to do is to stop thinking. Relax for once."

"I thought you normally didn't think."

"Very funny."

She adjusted her head on her grassy pillow.

"Or at the very least, let's think about something else."

Madison held her hand up, reaching for the stars.

"Do you think this is our first time being outside?" she asked.

"I thought we weren't talking about that anymore."

"We aren't. This is a different topic. I'm talking about being outside. Aren't the stars beautiful?"

"Yeah, I guess."

"This is a weird scenario for a first stargazing session."

"Weird seems to be our middle names. Everything we do is weird."

"Can't deny that."

There was a comfortable silence for a moment, each basking in the beauty of the view above them.

Inevitably, Madison's mind began to wander, and her mouth was opening before she could think.

"Jason?"

"Yeah?"

"Do you… feel like something's missing?"

Jason laughed, a comforting yet infuriating sound to Madison's ears.

"Yeah. Like my entire lifespan's worth of memories?"

"You know I don't mean that. I mean… someone. Someone important."

Jason went silent, considering his answer.

"Now that I think of it, yes. But unfortunately, the whole lost memory thing is preventing me from, well, remembering. Why do you ask?"

Madison considered telling him about the memory, but something inside her held her back.

"Nothing. Just a thought I had."

Jason looked at her, eyes squinting suspiciously.

"Oh well. I won't force you."

She sighed, deciding not to push it any further.

"We're supposed to be not thinking."

"I guess we're bad at it."

"Then maybe we should just go to sleep."

"I don't want to. I'm too awake."

"That was a dumb thing to say."

"Something that wouldn't be expected of me, I know."

"Alright, then. If you don't want to go to sleep, then answer something for me. What do you think of our powers?"

"What kind of question is that?" Jason asked, confused. Madison sighed, closing her eyes.

"Just answer it" she said, the mood suddenly sombre.

There was silence as Jason thought.

"I think they're very useful. For self defence, making jobs easier, and other things, but of course, that depends on how you use them."

"But do you think they're bad? Do you think we shouldn't've had them in the first place?"

Jason got up from his position, giving her a scrutinizing glare.

"Okay. Where is this coming from?"

Madison stayed quiet, fiddling with the string on her hoodie.

"I regained another memory when I was unconscious."

"Ah. That makes sense. Do you want to talk about it?"

Madison looked at Jason.

He was a comforting sight for her, one that never failed to calm her. One that was always there, and always would be. His wind tousled blonde hair was ruffled and dirty. Dark bags were under his worn eyes, standing out due to his light complexion. A caring smile adorned his features, and something swelled in Madison's chest. If he had been with her since the beginning, he deserved to be trusted with information.

Besides, he was the only one she had.

"I had a fight with a kid. There were others there, shouting things at me. Cheering the boy I was fighting with on. I lost, and just like that, they all left. That was it. And I remember being so angry, that I vowed that I wouldn't hold back my power on the next person I saw." She stopped, hanging her head down low.

"And did you do that?" Jason asked.

"Almost. Somebody came back into the room."

Jason pressed his lips together.

"And I'm guessing it wasn't me."

Madison shook her head.

"It was the person you were asking me about before, wasn't it?"

She nodded.

"It's just... I'm so mad at myself for almost hurting him. He was so kind to me, and I almost did something bad to him just because of the way I felt. The kids who called me a monster were all right. It would've been better if I'd-"

"Those kids weren't right about anything. From what I've heard, they didn't even get to know you. All they saw was that you were different, and that's what they went on. Perhaps they were a little scared, but who wouldn't be? It's you we're talking about."

"You got that right."

"Don't let any of the things they said about you get under your skin. I think we should be proud of who we are."

"Amnesiac kids who have strange unexplained powers?"

"Yes. Exactly that. But that's not all we are."

Madison smiled at him in a challenging way.

"Oh yeah? What else are we, then?" she asked.

"We can be whatever we want to be. Right now we're adventurers, mystery solvers, sorcerers, astronomers. But most of all- "

"Let me guess, transcenders?"

Jason looked at her, the humour gone and sincerity left behind.

"No. Most of all, we're human."

Madison closed her eyes, relishing the sound of that rolling off his tongue. Strangely enough, that was exactly what she wanted to hear.

"How do you do that?" Madison murmured, her eyes still closed.

"Do what?"

"Always make my worries and fears go away while still remaining a total nerd."

"It's talent. I should become a psychologist."

"Yeah, once we get off this island and figure out what the hell is going on."

"It's a plan."

"You ready to sleep now?"

"Yeah. It turns out that talking to you for a bit can trigger my brain cells to shut down from exhaustion."

"Rude."

"You're one to talk."

They lay down side by side, watching the stars and

feeling at ease for the first time in ages.

Madison felt her eyes slowly drifting off, not before she spotted a long shining streak blast across the sky. She smiled as she succumbed to sleep.

A shooting star.

* * *

Her footsteps were unconcealed and heavy as she ran down the corridor to the library. She didn't have to worry about anything on days like these. Not the other kids, the adults or getting caught.

Her favourite days were always when the Master came to teach them.

"I'm here!" she yelled, swinging the library door open with vigour and enthusiasm. The Master looked up at her from a book he and Jason were hunched over. Jason smiled at her excitedly, while the Master gave her a mock tut.

"I taught you better than to be late to my classes."

Madison huffed and walked over, insulted.

"Well maybe I had something better to do. You might not believe this, but you're not the centre of the universe."

The Master feigned shock, dramatically gasping and putting his hand to his chest.

"I had no idea!" he wailed.

"Let's start the lesson now" Jason cut in hurriedly, not wanting the drama to escalate.

Madison walked over to the desk they were sitting at, peering in over Jason's shoulder.

"What's that?" she asked.

"I was showing the Master the book I found on the transcenders. I wanted to get his opinion on its factuality and accuracy."

"It's mostly correct. However, the source appears to be quite biased when talking about certain aspects."

"Like what?" Jason asked.

"When dark mist first became present in the atmosphere, it wasn't completely the transcenders' fault. There was some… extra work involved."

"What kind of work?" Madison asked, intrigued.

The Master let out an audible sigh.

"It's quite long and complicated. I'm sure you'd get bored."

This only encouraged Madison even further.

"But I want to know!"

"Me too!" Jason added.

The Master shook his head, a smile playing on his lips.

"Fine, then. There was a rumour, years ago, of an occurrence."

The two leaned in closer, even more curious.

"What happened?"

"Nobody really knows exactly what happened. Most would compare it to a demonic possession, for lack of a better term."

Jason's eyes flew open.

"How did that happen?"

"An entity of some form took control of someone's body. This started the chain of events which led us to where we are now."

The Master shut the book with a bang, setting it on the table.

"But of course, that doesn't matter now. Let's focus on what I came here for. Lessons."

Madison and Jason looked up at him, buzzing with excitement.

"So what're we learning today? I don't care as long as it's cool."

"Actually, we're not training your powers today. I've decided to teach you about something else."

Both children visibly deflated after hearing that they weren't doing any magic.

"Then what's the point? Anything else is boring" Madison grumbled, crossing her arms.

The Master shook his head in exasperation.

"It's extremely important for you to know this. Even the most skilled people will never be at their best without knowing. I'm teaching you about yourself. How you're made up. Who you are and where you come from."

Jason raised his hand timidly.

"Actually sir, we already know how we're made up. We learnt that in biology."

"And we already know where we come from. Countries are a thing we learn in geography."

The Master pinched the bridge of his nose in exasperation.

"You kids will be the death of me. And that's an amazing feat, since I've managed to live this long."

He gave them both a stern look.

"Your biology classes haven't covered everything you need to know, Jason. And I'm not just talking about different countries, Madison. I mean the bigger picture. The universe."

Both their eyes widened, taking that in.

"Oh. That makes more sense."

"Jason, could you switch off the light, please?"

He stood up from his spot to do so. The room got sufficiently darker.

The Master held out his palm, and a golden glow emitted from it. The children watched, equally confused.

"You can both see the light coming from my hand, I'm sure. But do either of you know of its origins? Why I am able to do this?"

The two shook their heads.

"Alright. Let's go from the very beginning."

He snuffed the light, the room getting darker again.

The Master spread his arms far apart, and with the ease of painting a picture, projected an image from his fingertips.

The darkness was lit up with brand new hues, mixing together and becoming one. The image was small, but gave the impression of being everlasting, timeless, white dots glinting like jewels in the darkness. Madison and Jason stared in astonishment.

Maybe this lesson wouldn't be so boring after all, Madison thought to herself.

"This is the universe. It came from nothing, and is full of everything. It has no shape, no form, yet contains all forms of matter and energy. But there's a particular form that enables us to be who we are. We just call them Particles. They're what connect every single living thing together.

"Most believe that it's what gives us our powers. It's flowing through us right now, as we speak. But here's the thing. Each person, depending on their genetics, has a different amount of these Particles inside them. Most people have a tiny amount of this in their body, but there are those who have just a bit more than average. These are who people call transcenders, people like you or me."

Madison and Jason looked at each other, then the Master.

Questions ran rampant in Madison's mind.

"If this is true, why haven't I ever heard of it anywhere before?" Jason asked.

"People don't like to believe things unless there is concrete proof. It's just in our nature. Most people, even transcenders, don't acknowledge its existence because of the lack of evidence there is to back it up" the Master replied.

He turned to the projected image, his eyes focused.

"There are different kinds of Particles to be found in the universe. Six, to be exact. Life, death, oblivion, creation, knowledge and time. And for each Particle deviation, there is a Source. A wellspring of power from which each transcender's abilities derives from. Depending on the person, they can have a varied mix of Particles inside them."

"How are you supposed to know which ones you have?"

"Normally, you wouldn't. But sometimes, based on the types of powers you have, you can tell. Madison, you have mostly creation Particles, and Jason has mostly oblivion."

Madison looked at her hand, willing a faint blue glow to emerge.

"Where exactly do these Particles come from?" she asked.

It confused her. If everyone had these Particles in them, why was it such a big deal to others that she could draw power from them?

"That is beyond even my understanding, Madison. As far as we know, it came from the universe. And the universe came from nothing. I can only guess that the dust came from this too." Madison huffed, not satisfied with the explanation.

Jason blinked at the projected image of space, eyes devoid of emotion, staring indefinitely.

"But…what exactly is nothing? And where did it come

from?"

The Master fixed him with an amused stare.

"Look at you! Asking all these deep psychological questions! Although I am wise and knowledgeable, I don't know quite that much. And that is besides the point anyway."

Jason looked like he was lost in thought, and the Master regarded him worriedly. Madison did too.

He got like that sometimes, quite often actually. Like he was there, but only physically. He'd stare ahead of him, lost in his mind, and wouldn't be stirred unless you splashed a bucket of water in his face (that happened once).

"You told me about where we came from before, Madison. The answer to that is not confined to regional landmasses.

This is where we're from."

He widened his arms, the swirling image expanding as he did. Madison closed her eyes as the image soared past her, then feeling nothing, she opened her eyes. They flew open immediately.

It was like she had been transported to another world.

They were in space.

She and Jason gazed around in wonder and awe, marvelling at the sight of the universe.

Her heartbeat began to speed up from excitement, the dark yet colourful expanse triggering something inside her she hadn't felt since the night she had tried to escape the confinement building. She couldn't identify it then, but now she recognised it as an awareness of all the possibilities this life has to offer.

"You see, everything, absolutely everything is connected within the universe. We are made from literal stardust, which only deepens this link. There is something you always have to

remember if you want to be the best transcender you can be. Be reminded of it when you look out at night and see the stars, the vast expansive universe. This is where I come from, where my powers come from. Where everything and everyone came from. So we are all in the same."

The illusion faded, the multicoloured beauty of the universe fading to the dark, shabby library they were really in.

"People don't remember this. We've split ourselves into groups and forgotten all about the big picture."

Madison regarded the Master sadly, remembering the times she and the other kids had fought. She remembered looking out the only window in the building on the third flight of stairs.

Looking out to the sky.

She always saw nothing but inky black.

"But, how are people supposed to remember if they can never see the stars?" she questioned.

The Master regarded the children sadly, but with a strange glimmer in his eye.

"Then we'll just have to remind them."

He walked over to switch on the light.

"I suppose that concludes our lesson for the day. I hope I didn't bore you too much."

The children, dumbstruck, shook their heads.

The Master chuckled, leaning down to pick up his bag under the table.

"Here, a treat."

He handed them both something rectangular, covered in shiny golden foil. Madison recognised it as chocolate.

"Thanks!" Jason grinned, putting his in his pocket.

Madison teared hers open and wolfed it down as soon as the Master handed it to her.

"Thanks" she grinned, her mouth full. Jason shook his head, sighing.

"What were you expecting? This was my first chocolate in ages!"

"I don't know what I expect of you anymore" Jason grumbled.

He spotted another bar of chocolate lying on the table.

"Sir, could we have that one too, please?" he asked politely.

"What? Don't push your luck, mister! I'm not going to be giving you treats left right and centre now!"

Madison caught on to what he was doing, though she was unsure of whether she agreed or not.

"It's not for us! It's for a... friend."

The Master's eyes widened considerably.

"A friend? I didn't know you had those! In that case, of course."

Madison stuck her tongue out at him for the small insult, while Jason grabbed the bar from the table.

"Well, I must be going. Try not to get into too much trouble while I'm gone" the Master concluded.

"See you next time!"

"Good riddance!"

"See you, Jason. Good riddance to you too, Madison!" the Master gave her a stink eye while his particles dissolved into nothing. In a flash of bright light, he was gone.

Madison turned to Jason, her head tilted to one side.

"How does he manage to do that?" she asked.

"Do what?"

"Break into this place every time without a single person knowing. There's security everywhere here! And if he can easily break in, why can't we easily break ou-"

"Not this again!" Jason groaned, as they started on their way out of the library.

"I'm joking!" Madison swung the dusty double doors open, and they were in the hallway.

"Good, because I don't want a repeat of what happened last time."

" But, I wonder if we tried it again, would we be successful?"

"Madison-"

"Just think about it! Before, we were nine year olds without a proper plan-"

"I'm warning you-"

"Now we're older, and have more control over our powers-"

"Do you ever learn?" Jason groaned, slapping his hand over his face.

"I'm just saying!"

"Guys!" a friendly voice distracted them from their conversation.

Jason and Madison looked up, Jason breaking out into a grin, Madison's expression unwavering.

They stopped as he ran over.

"Where have you both been? I've been looking for you both for ages!"

The two shared a quick glance, Madison seeing a flash of guilt in Jason's eyes.

One of the terms of their agreement with the Master was to keep quiet about their training to everybody.

Even the kind boy who couldn't seem to leave them alone.

"Just reading in the library" Jason supplied, smiling a little too eagerly. He remembered what he had, reaching for his pockets.

"Look what we found!" he said as he showed him the bar.

"Chocolate? You found that in the library?" the boy said, eyeing it with amazement.

"It's for you" Madison stated blandly, in case it wasn't clear. The boy looked up at her.

"But what about the person who lost it? I'd feel really bad if they went back to the library only to find it missing. Chocolate is a really rare treat."

Madison and Jason looked at him, and then each other, with exasperated expressions on their faces.

" Just take it."

"I'm sorry, but I can't."

"Come on, you know you want it." Madison wafted the chocolate under his nose.

"Not at the expense of someone else loosing their treat."

Jason and Madison sighed, looking defeated.

"You're too good for your own good" Jason mumbled.

The boy smiled fondly at them, giving them both a pat on the shoulder.

"You don't have to worry about me, guys. I'm fine."

Madison frowned. This boy was a mystery to her. She couldn't think of a single reason why he was always so nice to them. For a while she'd believed it was pity, or curiosity.

But as time went by, she realised it could only be one thing.

This boy wanted to be their friend.

Nothing more, nothing less.

And if that was the case, she hoped with all her heart that it would stay that way.

"When you say that it makes me want to worry about you more."

"Reverse psychology" Jason added knowingly.

"Anyway, where were you guys going?" he asked.

"The dining hall" Madison answered.

"Let's hurry up so we don't get left with those awful 'All in One' packets." Madison shuddered, relieving the horrible slimy texture of one sliding down her throat.

"Actually, you guys go ahead. There's something I want to do first" Madison said, turning away from the two with a quick word of goodbye. The other two did the same, returning on their journey to the dining hall.

She went up a flight of stairs, then another, a strange feeling knotted in her chest. Why was she feeling nervous? She did this all the time.

Finally, she arrived. At the third flight of stairs.

The only window in the building.

She got up on her toes, cursing her height once more. Most of the children her age didn't need to do that to see.

Madison didn't know what she'd expected, but she saw the same sight that she always did.

Pitch black in the sky.

Not a cloud, not a ray of sunlight and not a hint of any other colours. This time, it made her sad.

She wanted to see the stars.

She recalled what the Master told her during their lesson. People would be reminded of where they come from if they could see the stars.

A strange idea came to her mind.

What if…she found the stars? Then everyone would remember. Everyone would be happier. And free. Free to do whatever they wished.

She leaned her cheek against the windowsill, imagining that.

A blue sky.

Stars at night.

And a wide world to explore.

It would all be possible if she could find the stars.

Maybe it was possible. With her training and newfound knowledge, she could do it.

It was only a matter of time.

"Madison!" a voice sounded from all around.

"Madison! Wake up!"

Wake up!

Wake up.

"Wake up!" Jason's frightened voice forced Madison's eyes open.

"What is it?" she asked sleepily, rubbing her bleary eyes. In her peripheral vision, she spotted a bright light in the direction of the forest.

"What's that?" she asked, the sleep suddenly leaving her.

"Right now, something just crashed from the sky."

"What?!" Madison yelped, jumping up from her spot.

As she shook away the last of her tiredness, she realised that it hadn't been a shooting star she'd seen earlier on.

"It caught fire, and then I heard something."

He leaned in closer, seriousness etched in his tone.

"Voices. We're not alone anymore."

CHAPTER 10

SHE DIDN'T KNOW WHAT SHE WAS FEELING AT THE MOMENT.

Fear, or excitement?

Haziness, or clear minded?

Either way, she stood up, buzzing full of new energy. For some reason, fear wasn't the strongest feeling in her mind at the moment.

Curiosity was.

"How close were the voices?" she asked.

"I'm not sure, but they shouldn't be able to hear us from here."

Madison gazed at the fire, a sense of intrigue filling her.

"Let's follow them" she said.

Jason stared at her as if she had gone mad.

"Do you hear yourself? No way we're doing that! We don't know where they came from, or what they're doing here."

"Exactly! And I thought we were meant to be looking for answers. They could provide us with some sort of info."

Jason sighed, his head in his hands.

"Why do I even bother" he grumbled, starting towards the forest. The fire in the distance died down, the pungent smell of smoke being the only thing that remained of it.

"We keep our distance. And if they see us, we're gone."

Madison grinned, following suit.

"Of course."

* * *

The forest looked different at night.

The trees appeared taller, and more menacing. Small sounds seemed heightened, adding to the gloomy atmosphere. And a compromising fear grabbed a hold of her as they traversed through the forest. So far, they hadn't heard any voices. But they found a scorched bit of earth not too far in.

"This is where the crash happened" Jason whispered, staring apprehensively. There was nothing else to see there, apart from the blackened ground.

The pulse of Madison's heart began to quicken. Seeing visible proof that there was somebody else there beside themselves was almost enough to make her think twice about her plan.

She shook her head, angry at herself. It wasn't like her to get scared by a bit of scorched earth.

It took a lot more than that.

Then the memory of the creature entered her mind, sending a deep chill down her spine.

"We can't just stand here and stare. We've got to catch up! Let's go!" she whispered, walking ahead. Jason rolled his eyes, following her.

It was a little later on until they saw them- blurry outlines of people not too far ahead. Jason grabbed her arm, mouthing the words.

Don't screw this up.

Madison rolled her eyes, ignoring the pulse of her heart.

And the instinct inside her telling her to turn back.

They stayed watching them from a distance, until Madison had had enough.

"Let's get close enough to hear what they're saying. We're not learning anything this way."

Jason looked at her, his gaze communicating even more than his words did.

"No way."

She sighed, looking ahead once more. She gasped, realising the people ahead of them had stopped.

And not at any random place.

At the giant hole.

Madison and Jason looked at each other, seeing the same bewilderment in each's expression.

The same spark of curiosity.

A silent agreement was reached to get closer.

They edged towards the trees, hiding behind one close enough to hear them, but not close enough to see properly. Inhaling cold night air into her lungs, Madison ignored the squealing urge inside her to escape, and instead she squinted, enough so that she could see the people she was following.

There were three of them, of varying heights, but that was just about all she could make out. But at least they were close enough to hear them.

"-is it? That's what you wanted to show us?" Madison picked up on the voice that was currently speaking.

"What's so special about a hole in the ground?" a voice, distinctly female spoke.

A male voice replied.

"This isn't just any random hole. It was created by somebody."

The third voice scoffed.

"Must have taken them years to shovel. It looks pretty deep."

"No, of course they didn't shovel it! A transcender did it!"

Madison and Jason looked at each other, intrigued by the conversation. Madison remembered the term transcender from her memory, and a jolt went through her.

There was a silence for a moment, the two children waiting for the strangers to speak.

"Did you see them do it?" the woman asked.

"Yes. I was there when it happened. Two kids. One of them stomped the ground, and a crack appeared. The ground just gave away."

That confused her. She knew that nobody else had been on this island. And she knew for a fact that nobody else was there when Jason created the hole as well.

The other two considered that for a moment.

An uneasy feeling twisted in Madison's gut. Something wasn't right. Well, less right than things normally were.

"Weird. Two kids, you say?"

"Yes."

"You mean like the two kids who are hiding behind the tree listening to our conversation?"

There it was.

Her heart stopped in her chest. Jason looked at her, saying the same thing that her gut was telling her to do.

"Run!"

That was all she needed. In a flash, she grabbed Jason's hand, sprinting in to the left.

"Where are you going?! Go the opposite way!"

"I can't! Then we'd reach the shore, and have nowhere to run!"

"Then where are you going?!"

"Hell if I know!"

On they hurdled, jumping over rocks, dodging trees, running through bushes, their clothes getting snagged by hanging branches.

Madison couldn't tell what was happening anymore. Everything was a blur. She couldn't feel her feet. Her eyes were misty and unseeing.

She stopped to take in deep breaths, her legs aching.

When she looked up, there were no signs of the three strangers.

"I told you this was a bad idea" Jason said between gasps.

"Well it's sort of your fault for agreeing to it. You know I never have good ideas!"

"I'm not going to argue about that now. We're literally being chased."

Madison leaned against a tree, breathing heavily.

"What do we do now? We can't go to the shore. We can't just wander around, hoping to not bump into them. Why am I so stupid? Why can't I just not screw things up for once?!"

Jason put a hand on her shoulder.

"Calm down. Getting worked up isn't going to help either."

He wore the distinct expression he got whenever he was working something out. His brows furrowed, his forehead creasing.

"Got anything?" Madison asked.

"Well, I can't really use my powers, since I still don't know how I did it the last time. And you can't use yours. I say we revert to plan we came up with earlier on. We find the Source. It might be a bit earlier than expected, but that won't matter as long as we find it."

Madison looked at him, the mood suddenly sombre, her heart beating faster in her chest for some reason.

"And what happens after that?"

"We find a way to get back."

"That's so unlike you. You normally wouldn't go ahead with a plan unless it's completely fool proof."

She sighed.

"But since it's the only thing we have, we might as well."

She got up from her leaning position against the tree.

"Do you still remember the way?" she asked.

She was grabbed by an unfamiliar hand.

Madison wasn't given any time to retaliate as it locked her hands behind her back. She struggled violently as the person kept her in a tight grip.

"There are easier ways to keep her still, Maia. Allow me."

Now that he was closer, Madison could finally see him.

He was the smallest of the three outlines she had spotted. He looked young, maybe a teenager. White blonde hair was combed away from his face, which she couldn't see very well in the dark.

Then she saw his eyes.

They were a shockingly vibrant violet, which seemed to glow in the darkness of the forest.

A forceful pulse surged through her entire body.

She couldn't move.

Or speak.

The woman let go of her.

"Thanks. She was getting annoying." She walked over to the boy's side.

She was older than the boy, though still relatively young. Her brown hair was long and bothersome looking, tied into a ponytail at her nape, and her eyes were considering her curiously, a piercing hazel.

The third man and Jason were nowhere to be found.

"First of all, we know this is a bad first impression. We're sorry for the inconvenience. Here, would you like a sweet?"

The boy held out what looked like candy in an aluminium wrapper. When there was no reply, he tucked it into one of the large pockets of her hoodie. This only served to infuriate her.

"Let's start again. Hi. The name's Lucas. This is Maia" he pointed to the woman, who only rolled her eyes.

"What's yours?"

Madison tried forcing her mouth open, but to no avail. Instead, she contented herself with trying to force all the hate that she had into one gaze.

Lucas realised his mistake.

"Oh, silly me."

With another in depth gaze, Madison found herself able to move her entire face again.

"Who the hell are you?! And what did you do to me?! Unfreeze me this minute!"

" I can't do that. We have to wait until Faolan comes back with your friend. You know him, right? Really tall? Really curly hair? Really dumb, sometimes?"

Madison narrowed her eyes once more, giving them a death glare.

"Where did you bring him?"

"Bring who? Faolan, or your friend?"

"You know who I'm talking about!"

"Your friend, then. He's the one that has the powers, right? I'm not gonna lie, I was kind of doubtful when Faolan told me about it. But now it seems clear that he was right."

Madison's curiosity won out over her anger.

"You weren't here before."

The woman, Maia, spoke up.

"We weren't. But Faolan was."

Madison's puzzlement was evident on her face, and this prompted Lucas' eyes to widen, as he made a realisation.

"She doesn't know."

"I don't know what?" Madison asked, annoyed but equally curious.

Lucas snickered, a sound that Madison never wanted to have the misfortune of hearing again.

"Don't worry about it. You'll find out soon enough."

Maia stepped forward, still staring at Madison intently.

"We should just leave her here, Lucas. She doesn't seem like she'd be of any use to us. We need to find it quickly."

Something clicked in Madison's mind and it became clear what these people wanted.

And of course it had to be the very same thing she was looking for as well.

The Source.

"So that's what you came for" she said out loud, the comment not going unheard to the other two.

"Are you talking about the Source?" Lucas questioned, getting closer.

She didn't answer, glad that she was right.

"Do you know where it is?"

No answer again.

"Well that's a shame. If you tell us, we could very easily unfreeze you."

Madison kept quiet, revelling in the fact that she had something over them.

Something that they really needed.

And when that was the case, deals could always be struck.

"I'll keep you frozen here until you tell me."

"Guess I'll be frozen for a while."

Maia pinched the bridge of her nose.

"This obviously isn't working. We need a different

approach."

Madison found her window of opportunity.

"You're right. Let's make a deal."

Maia's head lifted, a suspicious expression on her face.

"What kind of deal?"

"Simple. We trade information. You tell me about who you are and where you come from, and I give you the location of the Source."

The two considered this, looking at each other.

"Alright, little girl. You've got yourself a deal."

Madison bristled at being called a little girl, but she didn't let it get to her head. There were more important things to be worrying about.

She felt a wave of relief roll over her body as she was unfrozen. She fished around for the candy that Lucas had stowed away in her pocket. When she had it in her grasp, she pitched it into the depths of the forest as far as she could. Lucas gave her a unbelievable stare.

"How could you just throw away good candy?"

Madison looked back to Lucas and Maia, realising they were expecting her to start talking.

"I forgot to tell you one more thing."

"What's that?" Lucas asked.

Madison gave him a glare full of hatred and loathing. As if she would ever trust these people with her information.

Or people in general.

"I won't be doing anything for you until I find Jason."

With that, she took off with speed, faster than she ever had run before, feeling a strange sense of triumph. She ran, dodging nimbly past trees and hurdling over bushes.

She ran until they couldn't have possibly been able to catch up with her.

Stumbling to a stop, she gulped in some much needed air. If this event was following any of the patterns that her earlier escapades did, then something even worse was going to happen. She had learnt from this experience to trust her gut feeling from now on.

Just as she thought that, she turned around, only to find something that shocked her down to the core.

A dark cloud of black mist, exuding freezing winds rolling towards her.

Her insides clenched with the very same fear she had been running from this entire time.

CHAPTER 11

As I was dragged away by an unfamiliar rough hand to an unknown destination, all I could think of was how fierce the pain in my head was.

My agitation grew, and it burst out, seizing hold of my consciousness.

I howled, partly from the pain, partly because I was terrified and confused and had no idea what was going on.

At last we stopped, and I tripped and stumbled, crashing to the ground.

I found myself looking up at my kidnapper.

His face was pale and gaunt, a mess of unruly dark curls spiralling from his head. Glaring at me with sharp black eyes, he walked in front of me, leaning in close. Something about him was familiar, though I couldn't pinpoint it exactly.

"You're the one that made that hole, aren't you?"

His voice was gruff and deep, faintly accented.

I didn't answer. Knowledge and information could be the most powerful thing of all, sometimes. I gave mine sparingly.

He pulled me to my feet.

"Answering my question would be in your best interest."

He did something very unexpected.

It looked as if his entire body broke apart, bit by bit, forming smaller and smaller parts. I watched, dumbfounded, as the parts exuded a bright green light, reassembling, taking a different form.

The form of a wolf.

"You're..." I stuttered, completely forgetting about my headache. It pounded precariously now, as if something were about to burst out.

The wolf circled around me, sizing me up most probably.

"Did you create the hole?"

The pain in my head grew, and I responded quickly.

"I don't know!"

"Don't play dumb with me! Your kind think you know everything. That you're better than average. That silly name you've given yourselves doesn't change a thing about what you're really like."

My head pounded even harder. It was getting hard to breathe.

"I can't-"

"Oh, I'm sure you can. You just don't want to. Now tell me! You're wasting my time!"

And that was it. That was the last straw.

If I were to describe the sensation that I felt when I heard the voice, I'd say it resembled an explosion of pain.

He's right, you know.

"What? Who's that?!"

Who I am isn't important. The wolf is right. You don't want to know who you are. But it's essential, to me, to us, that you do.

Despite the dangers, I was intrigued by what the voice was saying.

"Then what am I?"

That depends. What do you want to be?

"I...don't know."

Alright, I'll phrase it differently. What do you need to be?

"I...I need to be strong."

Then what you need to be is nothing. Nothing is the strongest thing of all. Everything that was ever created came from it. So if you're nothing, you could be everything.

How am I supposed to do that?

I can help you.

How?

How is besides the question. Just trust me.

And... you promise to make me strong, to protect

Madison?

Sure, sure. Whatever you want. We have a deal?

…yes.

The last thing I remember is my world fading to black, and a dark mist enveloping me.

* * *

Nothing.

What is it?

Where does it come from?

Does it even exist?

I think it does.

I am nothing.

And I exist.

At least, I think I do.

If nothing is nothing,

how was everything created from it?

Does that mean nothing can be created from nothing?

I'm tired.

And I'm so cold.

My head hurts.

I don't think I like being nothing very much.

Can I be something now?

* * *

I woke up with a pounding headache, but as soon as it came, it disappeared.

I was in the forest again. I couldn't see anything. It was so dark. As I slowly came to my senses, I realised that I couldn't remember anything that had happened after the run in with the wolf.

It was strange. Something about this dark mist seemed familiar.

Oh no…was the mist creature coming back again?

Wasting no more time, I shakily stood up to my feet.

The darkness closed in on me, consuming me whole.

Where was Madison? Was she okay?

Where was the wolf and the other two we had been following?

How did things go so wrong?

I could feel my heart pounding in my chest. The beginnings of a sob hacked up in my throat.

Determined, I wiped my tears away forcefully.

I would not let fear hinder my progress.

I chose a direction to walk in.

I walked.

And I walked.

And I walked.

The whole time, I repeated the mantra in my head.

This is fine, this is fine, this is fine.

This was definitely not fine.

Everywhere I went, it felt like a million different eyes were spectating silently from the shadows.

How did this happen?

"Jason!"

A familiar voice broke me out of my stupor.

"Madison!" I yelled, stumbling blindly, running to the sound of the voice.

"Jason? Jason!" she replied, most likely doing the same.

I heard the sound of leaves crunching underfoot, and I knew she was closer.

Without delay, she was right in front of me, and enveloped me in a hug. I gripped her tightly.

"I thought I wouldn't find you!"

"Me too!"

The excitement dying down, I held onto her hand, unwilling to let go.

"Do you have any idea what the hell's going on?" she asked, confusion adorning her features.

I blinked, having forgotten about the situation we were in with the joy of finding Madison.

"No clue. I just woke up, and suddenly there was all this dark mist. I was so scared!"

"Wait. You just woke up?" Madison's expression was one of bafflement and then anger as she grabbed me by the shoulder and shook me.

"What did that jerk do to you? If I get my hands on that-"

"It wasn't him! It happened by itself. Suddenly I had this headache, and then I just blacked out."

"What? Are you okay?"

"Yeah, I'm better now.."

I touched my forehead, just to check. No lingering pain remained to indicate that it had ever happened.

"What do we do?"

Madison looked at me sternly.

"Well, you said it before. We go find the Source."

She looked out into the enhanced darkness of the forest.

"It's not that dark. We could still find the way."

I sighed, some of the weight from earlier alleviating now that Madison was here.

"You're right. We should get going, then."

In the darkness, I barely saw Madison give me a shaky smile.

* * *

The walk through the forest was slow, as I would occasionally get mixed up with the direction. But other than that, it was quiet.

"The wolf" I said.

Madison looked at me.

"What about it?"

I took in a large breath, unsure of how I should arrange my words. "One of the people we saw. He…turned into it. He was the wolf the whole time. "

Madison spluttered.

"What?!" she yelped. Her grip on my hand tightened, and I knew it was from anger.

It usually was with her.

"So that's what they were telling me about."

"Who?"

"Lucas and Maia. Those are the other twos' names. And the wolf is called Faolan. I should've known from the moment they hinted it."

I frowned. "I don't see how you could have."

"And they have powers as well. Lucas did, at least."

I felt my body go rigid for a second.

"What did he do?"

"His eyes were a weird purple colour. When I looked at him, my entire body froze."

"What?! How did you escape?"

I couldn't see her face, but I could hear her chuckle.

"I tricked them. It was a lot easier than I thought it would be."

We continued like that for a while. Eventually, I came to

a stop at a raised slope.

"We've just got to go over that," I clarified, "and then we should be at the waterfall."

"Alright."

We clambered over it, and sure enough, the same sight that we had been greeted with yesterday was in front of us right now.

Just darker, and less inviting.

I saw the lake we had played and splashed in earlier.

It looked bottomless and ice cold.

I would never dream of jumping in there now.

"Come on" Madison urged me, suddenly eager.

That was strange. She was so reluctant to find the Source earlier on.

We walked across to the great gushing waterfall.

"Those guys from earlier are here because they're looking for the Source" Madison said.

I spluttered.

"Really? You could have told me that before! Did you tell them that you knew where it was?"

Madison chewed her bottom lip, looking somewhat guilty.

"Well, only indirectly. They kinda just assumed."

I paled. I knew what kind of trouble this could spell for us.

"That means that they're probably looking for you right now!"

"I know! That's why I want to get to it as quickly as possible. Aside from the whole secret cave thing, it's kinda hard to miss."

"You should be more careful with these kinds of things next time."

Madison scoffed.

"Trust me, there won't be a next time."

I hoped there wouldn't be. But right now there was one thing we needed to do.

We got to the waterfall, the crashing of the water as deafening as before.

Madison automatically gripped my hand tighter, unwilling to express her fear out in the open.

I knew what a hard ordeal this would be for her. I admired her bravery.

"Remember, I'll be here with you this entire time."

Madison looked at me, a hardened edge to her stare.

"That's what I'm afraid of."

We descended in.

The cave was pitch black, apart from the tiny sliver of light which was only just viewable. Madison and I walked towards it like it was the only thing keeping us going.

And if I was being completely honest, it was.

The light got brighter and brighter. Soon little specks of blue dust were visible, floating all around, bringing with them tiny pinpricks of light.

"You feeling anything?" I asked.

Madison shook her head, her gaze fixed on the floor.

"Just hold on to my hand, and tell me when you do. Even the slightest twinge."

Madison didn't answer me.

"Madison?"

No answer.

"Can you hear me?"

Her footsteps began to accelerate, and soon she was nearing a fast run.

"Madison, hold on-"

She yanked her hand out of my grasp, bolting forward.

"Madison!"

"Leave me alone!" she growled back. I paled.

This wasn't going to end well at all if I didn't do something quick.

"Wait!"

I grabbed her hand. She looked back at me, a hateful glare lighting her features.

But that's not what was unusual.

Her eyes had a glowing blue tinge to them, blue dust spiralling from her fingertips.

This was bad. I knew if she went to the Source in this state, nothing good would come of it.

Her expression was the most menacing yet as she uttered.

"Don't get in my way."

Chapter 12

The Source.

She'd finally found it.

She and the Source were one. Nothing, nobody could take it away from her.

Her life.

Her happiness.

Her freedom.

But this one seemed to think that he could. She scoffed. Didn't he realise she was more powerful than he could ever imagine?

"Move."

The boy didn't shrink away. Instead, he stood up taller, holding his ground.

All he was accomplishing was wasting more of her precious time.

"Madison, if you want to get the Source, you can't let this happen to you. Remember who you are."

What in the world was he talking about? This was who she is. This was her true state.

He would never understand.

Dealing with him was a waste of time. She walked past him, boosting her speed to get to the Source.

"No!" he screamed, running in front of her again, spreading his arms out wide so she couldn't get past.

Her frustration grew.

"I said get out of my way!" she screamed, her eyes flashing dangerously. The blue dust which had been aimlessly floating around the cave picked up speed, whirring around her in a frenzied dance.

She glanced at her left hand, finding that it was glowing blue. She smiled. At last her power was coming back to her!

She thrust her hand forward, the swarm of dust soaring past her with speed. The entirety of it formed an enormous mass to knock Jason off his feet, sending him hurtling across the cave.

She laughed at the sight of him flailing aimlessly in the air, powerless.

She waited for the knock of the impact, the sight of a broken body falling down the side of the cave.

It never came.

But something far more disconcerting happened.

Dark mist exuded from the boy's chest, spreading around him, safely carrying him down from the height.

As he landed safely on the floor, the mist escaped from his body. It swirled and shifted, never conforming to the same shape.

She shivered at the sight, unsure why.

The mist took the form of a human, distinct facial features almost visible, but shifting constantly.

She stopped, absolute fear and confusion taking over her.

"What are you? What just happened?"

The strange human- looking creature watched her- then burst out laughing.

It was an unsettling sight for her to see, like laughing wasn't something that an entity of that form did often, or should do.

"You were miss brave and bold just a minute ago! While you were flinging around my host! Looks like things aren't always what they seem at first."

It drifted closer to her, leaving the boy lying on the floor. From what she could see, he was still alive, his chest rising and falling steadily.

The creature swirled around her, dark mist trailing behind it as it examined her closely.

"So you're the one he wanted to protect" it murmured under its breath.

"Get away!" she said, hating having it so close to her, the feeling of unease and fear and being...

Powerless.

That's right. That's why she was here. She needed to get to the Source.

She found an opening in the swirl of mist, dodging through, running towards the bright light.

She was almost there. Once she was, she would have it all.

Power.

Magic.

Freedom.

"Just where do you think you're going?" the voice of the creature rose behind her.

"You should've listened to what Jason said. You need to control yourself. Get rid of the urges your creation Particles are causing. That's the only way the Source will accept you."

Accept. What did that have to do with this? They were one. So she didn't have to wait for it to accept her.

As far as she was concerned, they had already chosen each other.

She took a running leap towards the light, but something dark came behind her and snatched her at the last moment.

"What kind of Source vessel are you, anyway? I thought you trained for this."

She still struggled defiantly, not giving up hope in the slightest.

"Well, you've given me no other choice. I'll have to do this the hard way."

A cold sensation left her body shaking with a horrible chilling feeling, causing her to stop struggling.

Her senses began to leave her.

As she closed her eyes and slumped to the floor, she saw a blurred outline of Jason's body lying on the ground..

The magnitude of what she'd done finally reached her at that moment.

I'm so sorry.

* * *

"I'm so sorry !"

Jason's anguished voice rises over the howling wind in your ears. The cold is everywhere, biting into you from all angles.

But this isn't on your mind now.

Jason is.

Or whatever that is.

Half of his face is consumed by dark shadows, swirling menacingly where his skin should be.

His expression is full of fear and sorrow as great rolls of tears slip down his cheeks.

"I'm sorry, I'm so sorry, I didn't mean to-"

The gravity of your situation hits you with the smash of icy winds in your face.

This is real, this is real and you're outside and it's cold and Jason turned into a monster-

"I so sorry! I'm sorry-"

And he was here and now he's gone and it's cold, so cold-

Jason's wails turn into hacking sobs, rising up over the howls of the wind once more-

You should have listened, should have stayed-

"Come back, come back! I didn't mean to-"

You turn your head in Jason's direction, your face stuck in a position of fear and shock as he he stares back at you, the tears still falling.

His eyes are luminous in the dark, but they are not the eyes you looked into everyday, the eyes you trusted more than anything in the world.

They aren't Jason's eyes.

They are someone else's.

Your mouth opens before you can stop it.

"Who are you?"

* * *

Madison's eyes opened to the flower strewn ceiling of the cave.

She sat up stiffly and painfully, addressing the ache in

her legs. All remembrance of pain left her when she saw Jason lying on the floor. Panic filled her, and she remembered exactly what had happened to get them both to this point. She glanced around in a frenzy, looking for the black mist that had emerged from Jason's body. There were no signs to be seen of it.

"Jason!" she cried, stumbling over to him.

He looked relatively fine, apart from a new gash on his hoodie which she had undoubtedly created.

There was no reply from him.

She shook him vigorously, praying that he was just resting.

A strangled sound came from his lips. She gasped.

Jason's eyes fluttered open, staring around in a disoriented state.

"Madison, I-"

"Jason!" Madison gave him no time to reply, wrapping him in a hug.

"I'm so sorry, I had no idea what I was doing and I couldn't control myself and I can't believe I let this happ-"

"Hold on. What are you talking about? I'm okay, but what happened?"

Madison gaped at him. How did he not remember?

Then she relieved the strange creature formed from mist rising out of his body, causing her to jolt in fear.

She thought of something.

Jason told her that he woke up not having any memories...right after the huge roll of mist came from the forest.

The roll of mist looked distinctly like the dark creature

they had seen in the forest earlier on in the day. Which he hadn't been affected by.

And it had happened while Jason was away…

"Madison? What is it? What happened?" Jason asked, worry filling his voice now.

Madison gave him a forced smile, unwilling to show any signs of what she had thought.

She decided that it would be too much for him to handle, especially since he had no clue what was going on, and the last thing she wanted to do now was to worry him even more.

Besides, she didn't know for sure that it was true.

"Don't worry. Nothing really happened. I just got a bit carried away."

A bit carried away wasn't exactly how she'd describe it. She'd almost killed him.

Jason narrowed his eyes at her, not believing her in the slightest, but not wanting to dig further into it.

"As long as everything's fine, then."

He gave a little gasp as he realised something.

"You're not reacting to the Source anymore!"

Madison glanced behind her, at the light. It shone radiantly, blinding her eyes. But the tug in her stomach to go to it wasn't as strong. She remembered the icy sensation that had taken over as the mist lulled her to unconsciousness.

"Strange" she simply replied, hiding a shiver.

Jason watched her, still not convinced that everything was okay.

"What are you waiting for? Aren't you going to get it? Those guys could be on our trail, so we need to be quick."

"I guess I have to, then."

Madison stood up, turning around to the Source.

Her legs turned to jelly as she shielded her eyes from the bright blue light. The tug in her gut became stronger the closer she got, but not as strong as it had previously been.

Why was that?

What exactly did that strange mist do to her?

She walked past the stalagmites and stalactites glowing with bright blue flowers to get to her destination at the edge of the cave.

The light was so bright and pure here that not even shielding her arm over her eyes could protect her.

She just stood there and stared, partly marvelling the glowing blue light, partly wondering what the heck she was supposed to do next.

Instinctively, she reached out her hand, to touch it.

An age seemed to pass as she reached for it, the world slowly fading away, until it was just her and the light.

Her and the Source.

Then there was the moment of connection.

That was the moment where everything changed.

Power built up inside her, filling the empty hole in her core.

She was overwhelmed, but at the same time, she needed more.

More.

More.

Her eyes only saw blue, blue of varying colours. Blue of every shade, shining before her eyes, electrocuting her body, filling her to the brim.

With power.

As soon as it had begun, it was over. The cave returned to its normal colour, as if nothing had ever happened.

She felt…

how did she feel?

Relatively normal. To be honest, she didn't feel any different.

"Madison! Are you alright?"

She blinked as Jason ran towards her.

"Yeah. I guess."

"What's that?"

"What?" she questioned, looking to where Jason stared at her palm. She was holding a misshapen stone, glowing haphazardly.

"What the hell is this?" she asked, staring at the stone in puzzlement.

Jason stared at it in awe.

"Isn't it obvious? It's the Source!"

She looked at it strangely. The stone didn't look out of the ordinary, apart from the dim glow it held. Madison had been expecting a bright glowing ball, crackling with energy. Not this sad rock.

She gave it a three out of ten.

"It's cool that we found it and all, but to be honest, I'm disappointed."

Jason grasped her arm, beaming at her.

"Why? Don't you see? We finally have the Source! The thing we've been here to do this entire time! Now all we have to do is figure out how to use it, and then we're off this island. We can finally get more answers!"

Madison smiled weakly at him, knowing that it wasn't

going to be as simple as that.

Nothing ever was.

She watched as Jason picked a blue flower growing from a vine coiling around a stalagmite. This time, it didn't disintegrate at his touch, like they had before.

"When I touched them, they fell apart."

"Things must be changing, then. Here" he said, handing her the flower. It fit neatly on her palm, still glowing as brightly as before.

Madison allowed herself to smile, saving it in the deep pocket of her hoodie.

He was right. They had gotten this far. Now there was only a small stretch left.

"Who do we have here?"

A voice boomed around the cave, heightened by the echo that was provided by the high walls. Madison jolted, dropping the Source.

It fell, a tinny sound coming from it as it made contact with the ground. Her first thought was of the dark mist creature, but she knew it wasn't.

This voice was different. It had a high, tinkling tune with a dark undertone, reverberating all around them.

Madison's hand instantly found Jason's, squeezing tight.

"I asked you a question! What do you think you're doing!?" the voice demanded angrily, getting louder.

Madison looked down to the stone she'd dropped, putting two and two together.

She picked it up, holding the Source out.

"It's this you want, isn't it? You can take it back. We didn't want it anyway. It's more trouble than it's worth."

There was silence for a moment.

"You don't understand, do you?"

The glow of the Source got brighter and brighter, until Madison could barely see in front of her.

She dropped it hastily in surprise.

An array of blue dust exuded from the Source, swirling in an upward spiral, brighter than any other light in the cave.

At this point, Madison was getting worried for her eyes.

The outline took the form of a human, and in another bright flash, a girl floated in front of her.

She seemed tangible, but there was a transparent sheen to her body. Every ounce of her was some shade of blue glowing abundantly, from her dress, her cloak and her piercing eyes. Artic hair floated around her in waves, never still. Her expression was deadpan, curious, but predominantly angry.

She drifted closer to them, her brows furrowing.

"Two kids, huh? Mind explaining to me what's going on?"

"We came for the Source. We had no intention of bothering you" Madison answered hurriedly.

"You do realise that you can't do one without doing the other? What exactly do you need the Source for?"

Madison and Jason stared at each other. Apart from knowing it was the key to getting back, neither quite knew the answer.

The apparition watched Madison, her eyes narrowing dangerously.

"Wait a minute-" she edged in closer, Madison scooting back a little bit.

Her eyes widened with shock, then narrowed down in anger.

"No way."

Madison was beyond confused.

"Is… there a problem?" she asked, looking at the girl with timid confusion.

The girl let out a hearty laugh, its hollow sound resounding through the cave, sending chills down Madison's spine.

"Oh there is a problem! The biggest problem I've had to face in a long time!"

She floated towards her, giving her a beady glare.

"That would be you. You're the problem."

Madison felt her heart thud faster in her chest. She had no idea what was going on, and quite frankly, it was scaring her royally.

" I'm…not really following."

"Great! And she doesn't even know what she's done! How am I supposed to work with this?!"

Jason, who had been silent for a while, finally spoke, his voice wavering slightly from fear.

"I'm sorry, but if we're bothering you, we'll just be going."

The girl finally noticed him standing there, and a surprised smile lighted up her features.

"I would love for you to be able to do that. But unfortunately, that isn't physically possible anymore. Thanks to your friend over here who decided to meddle with things she didn't understand."

Madison felt her blood boil. It wasn't her fault that she didn't know what was going on!

"Look, finding the Source was what I was brought here to do, and I'm sorry that I don't understand what's happening, but maybe that's because nobody thought to explain it to me! And for the record, I also have no idea what's going on now, either!"

The minute the words came out from Madison's lips, she knew she'd made a grave mistake.

The girl's eyes turned stormy, flashes of a deeper blue sparking inside of them.

"Okay, little girl. You're officially on my bad side. And that's a bad state to be in, considering our circumstances."

Madison stepped back obligingly while Jason spoke up again.

"We're again extremely sorry for all of this, but what she said was true. We woke up here with no memory. All we knew was that we had to find the Source."

She examined them closely, seeming to stare somewhere beyond their physical appearance.

"So you're both transcenders. What're your names?"

"I'm Jason, and she's Madison" Jason said quickly, not giving Madison any time to talk.

"The name's Clover, by the way."

"Nice to meet you" Jason replied with a shaky smile.

The apparition, Clover, smiled at him back.

"You too. At least one of you has manners."

Madison did her best to ignore that.

"If what you said was true, there's going to be a lot more I need to explain to you. Let's get going."

Madison felt her eye twitch.

"You're coming with us?!"

Clover gave her the deepest death glare yet, turning her insides to ice.

"Yes, because of you. Trust me, if it were my choice, I would not be leaving. Now I suggest you quit your whining, because we have a whole lot to get through."

Not wanting to be scolded by her again, Madison walked towards the exit, picking up the Source. Jason followed behind her.

"Since you claim to have your memories wiped, there's a lot I'm going to have to explain. I'll start with the most basic of concepts."

Both children looked up at her expectantly, waiting for her to speak.

She turned to Madison.

"You. What you've just done is become the vessel for the Source of creation."

Madison felt her heart race, for no apparent reason at all.

"The what?"

CHAPTER 13

CLOVER SIGHED, PINCHING THE BRIDGE OF HER NOSE.

"I'll use an analogy. Kids like you understand those things, right?"

Madison nodded slowly, unsure of what else she should do. Jason watched the glowing apparition with awe. Of course he would be interested rather than cautious.

"Think of yourself as a cup. The Source is a drink. You just poured the drink into yourself. Was that easy enough for you to understand?"

Madison nodded begrudgingly, annoyed at the fact that she'd insulted her at least twice. Apparently, the Source's power was inside her. But she didn't feel any different.

Her mind wandered to the earlier events.

"Why was I the only one who got affected by the Source

before? Jason didn't."

Clover sighed.

"Okay, listen. I'm not going to explain this again, or in detail, because I'm tired and this is getting on my nerves."

She looked at them expectantly.

"You have Particles inside you. Those Particles enable you to use your powers. There are different types of these Particles. Everyone has varying amounts of each inside them. One of these types is creation."

She jabbed at Madison's stomach, which earned her a yelp. She hadn't expected Clover's body to have a tangible presence.

"Most of your Particles are the same type as the one making up the Source, which means you are eligible to become a vessel for the Source of creation. Have you got it? If not, too bad. I'm not explaining that again."

Madison rubbed her sore stomach, thinking over that whole idea again. Strangely enough, it made sense. None of it seemed too daunting to her, probably because she heard some of it from the Master in the memory she regained.

"So… the reason I didn't react to the Source is because I don't have a lot, or any creation Particles inside of me?" Jason asked, staring into space in thought.

Clover beamed gratefully at him.

"At least I'm getting through to someone!"

Madison bristled silently. She understood it as well.

"Subsequently, what was happening when you got near to the Source was your creation Particles reacting with it."

"What *is* the Source?" Madison asked.

"It's exactly what it sounds like. Nothing more, nothing less."

She frowned. That didn't really tell her much about it.

"How exactly did I become the…vessel?"

"It happened the moment you reached your hand to the Source. Your Particles and the Particles in the Source merged. But you're not able to use its power at the moment."

"Why?"

"You've blocked off your powers."

"What do you mean? How did I do that?"

"I don't know. You did it yourself."

There was a short pause. Madison stared at the stone in her hand. Before, its glow was weak and dim. Now it blazed, providing a source of light for them. The further they got away from the chamber, the darker it got.

"What are you, though? I mean, you just popped out of the stone like nobody's business. Are you, like, the soul of the Source or something weird like that?"

Clover gave her a beady glare, which insinuated that she would murder her if ever given the chance.

"No. I'm the Source guardian. Which is also exactly what it sounds like. That stone you're waving around like a flashlight contains all the energy of the Source, condensed into one tight spot. It's extremely important, so I suggest you keep it in a safe place and don't loose it."

At this point, the cave was almost completely dark. She wouldn't have been able to see at all if it wasn't for the Source, and Clover's glowing aura.

She wondered what they would do from this point on.

How she would be able to use the stone.

"So, what kinds of things can I do with this?"

Clover gave her a deadpan stare.

"It's literally in the name. The Source of creation? If you still don't get the hint, it can create things."

Madison felt her blood boil at her snarky comment.

"Look, the whole "becoming the vessel" thing was an accident. I didn't know it would mean this, and I'm sorry. But it doesn't mean that you should keep picking on me for no apparent reason!"

From the glow of the Source, she saw Jason give her a look which exuded a sense of 'bad idea!'

She also got a sense of that as well when she saw the expression on Clover's face.

"Oh! Well I'm sorry that because of your cluelessness, I get stuck teaching a toddler how to use their power instead of a fully trained, fully grown transcender! You may not care in the slightest, but you've just made my life a hundred times harder!"

Madison, not one to be put down by a display of anger, retaliated just as angrily.

"Same here! I can't believe I have to put up with you for the unknown future!"

"Me either! You make me sick!"

"No! You make me sick!"

"You can't say that because I already did!"

"Well guess what?! I said it anyway!"

"Guys! That's enough!"

Jason interrupted their shouting match, exasperation evident in his tone.

"We're not going to get anywhere like this. You've only

known each other for a few minutes yet you're already at each other's throats. Just…try establish a good relationship with each other. If you're going to be together for the unknown future, it will be worth it."

Madison shivered at the reminder, folding her arms together and looking the other way.

Not acknowledging her presence was a better idea in her opinion.

Clover seemed to decide the same thing.

Silence reigned over the cave.

Jason sighed.

"I said you should get to know each other better, not completely ignore each other. That'll just make it worse."

Madison looked at Clover begrudgingly.

"I don't want to talk to her. And I don't want to be the vessel either. We can just find somebody else to do it when we get back."

"Glad you feel the same way. I'm outta here."

The apparition disappeared in a flash of light.

Jason looked at Madison in annoyance.

"Did you seriously have to do that?" he spat.

"Do what? Be my normal self? Is that enough to make people hate my guts? Because it seems like that's all it takes!"

Jason took her hand, the blue stone illuminating the softening expression on his face.

"Come on now. That's not true and you know it."

Madison's eyes were dull and staring as she looked at him.

"Then explain, Jason. Tell me why everywhere I go, I end up doing something wrong to make people hate me.

Is it them, or me?!"

Without a word, Jason stopped right then and there in the middle of the cave. He drew Madison into a tight hug. Madison went limp for a minute, then hugged him back eagerly, relishing his warmth, the familiarity and safety of his arms around her.

"Stop saying that. It isn't true." His voice was quiet and reassuring, instantly calming her as well.

"I'm so sorry" she whispered.

"About what?" he asked, but he got no answer. Instead, she just held on tighter. They stayed like that a while longer, Madison unwilling to leave the tranquillity of the moment.

"Are you ready yet?" Jason asked.

Madison shook her head, but sighed anyway.They had to.

"Let's go."

Jason nodded, and together they continued on their way out of the cave.

Soon they could see the outline of the exit, even though it wasn't as clear as it should have been.

Madison had waited to see the night sky sprinkled with stars, but instead, saw the dark mist drifting around, and concealing them from view. This gave her a harsh reminder of the gravity of their situation.

Something told her that staying here for an even longer while wouldn't be such a good idea.

Madison saw the flash of the stone in the pocket of her hoodie, and Clover re- emerged, looking strangely alert.

"What happened here?" she asked, strict for some reason.

She didn't look in Madison's direction.

"We don't know" Jason answered. "Something must have happened while I was unconscious, but when I woke up, there was mist everywhere."

Madison felt guilty then. Maybe, just maybe, she'd been overreacting and Jason really didn't have anything to do with this.

Then she remembered seeing the dark mist emerge from his body, and she knew there was no excuse to evade the fact that Jason had caused this.

"This isn't good" the apparition said, drawing out a long breath.

"What does it mean?" Jason asked, a genuinely worried expression on his face.

Madison was conflicted.

Should she tell him?

Or would it just make things even more confusing for him? Perhaps she was over thinking this. He had faith in her, so she needed to have a little faith in him. Maybe it wasn't going to end up as that much of a big deal and Jason could find a way to reverse it.

 Yeah, that sounded alright. It wouldn't be of any notice to them at all after that.

Then the mist creature's voice resonated in her mind and she realised that perhaps it wouldn't be as easy as she had convinced herself it would be.

But either way, she'd have to tell him.

"Jason, there's something I need to tell you. It's kind of important-"

"Watch out!" Clover yelled, shoving her and Jason down to the ground. A large banging sound resounded all around them. It was so loud and so close, like lightning clapping in the sky just above them.

"What in the hell was that?!" Jason screamed, only just within earshot of Madison.

She probably knew.

"It's those guys. They followed us."

And sure enough, it was. The three figures walked towards them, only just visible through the dark mist.

"I must say, Madison, was it? You've really made our job much easier. And for that, I thank you."

It was the boy, Lucas speaking, with an already recognisable wide grin on his face.

Madison made a growling sound not very different to a wolf.

"You're not taking the Source."

He let out a little chuckle, only serving to infuriate Madison even more.

"It's not like you'll have a say in the matter either way. Just hand it over, and no harm will come to you. Or your friend."

Madison gritted her teeth. She knew that she absolutely could not give it to them, no matter what. She saw Jason tense in the corner of her eye.

"I'll try use my powers again. There's not much else we can do."

Madison grabbed his hand.

"No! You can't!" she shouted, and this only earned her two confused stares, from Jason and Clover.

"Why not?" he asked, confused.

"The ground might still be unstable from the hole you made" she lied smoothly.

"We're still here!" Lucas called, just to remind them. Even from where she was, she could see the flash of an aluminium wrapper in his hand. Madison felt her face form a scowl.

Clover rolled her eyes.

"You're making too big of a deal out of this, guys." Madison blinked at her.

Too big a deal? She thought they were being relatively calm, especially after narrowly avoiding an explosion.

"What do you suggest then?" she asked, hoping that she might come up with something useful.

"Easy. Just hold on to the stone and I'll help you."

Weary, but lacking in choices, Madison did as she was told.

"Oh well. I guess you've chosen the hard way" Lucas said from far away.

Everything happened at once.

Madison's arm, the one that was gripping the stone, turned a dastardly shade of blue, electricity cackling and popping inside of it. As if it were moving on its own, it thrust itself out and a bright blast or surge of energy shot out.

She panicked, drawing her hand back.

"What are you doing?!" Clover shouted, her voice pounding through Madison's head.

"I can't!" she shouted back, shutting her eyes fiercely.

Simultaneously, a deafening crack of thunder clapped in the sky directly above them. It was chaos.

She heard a scream, loud and frightful.

It wasn't hers.

Madison opened her eyes again, to find everything

desolated.

The surrounding area was back to the way it was before, the dark mist swirling around as it had been, refusing to go away even after all that had happened.

Madison's eyes darted around with a newfound alertness.

Jason was nowhere to be seen. The other three had also disappeared. Madison looked in her palm, the Source still embedded in it.

"Clover?"

The apparition reappeared, shedding light onto the otherwise dark surroundings.

"Clover! What just happened? Where's Jason? What in the hell is going on?!"

"I need you to calm down-"

"How can I calm down if my best friend has just gone missing without a trace?! Where is he? Did they take him?!"

She walked down towards the direction of the woods, calling wildly. Eventually, she had to give the search up. It was getting her nowhere, and inevitably only making her even more desperate.

Clover stared down at her, something like pity in her eyes.

"Are you done yet?"

Madison turned to her, anger spurring her to act.

"You! I thought you were going to fix things! Why the hell did you just do that?!"

"If you'd just listened to what I said, then this wouldn't've happened. Perhaps if you actually looked properly, you'd see what I've done instead."

She pointed in the direction of the woods.

Madison's eyes widened considerably.

There was a perfect trail of blue dust leading to the woods.

"Since you didn't comply when I tried to use the Source, we'll have to settle for this instead. It should lead us right up to them. And it's only visible to our eyes. No thanks needed."

Madison gazed at the apparition with apprehending excitement and a tiny bit of guilt.

"Right. Sorry about that."

Clover sighed, shaking her head.

"Oh well. It can't be helped. Next time, you'll have to trust me. Listen to exactly what I say. Let's get going, shall we?"

"Yeah."

They left the clearing, Madison with a newfound respect for Clover, and Clover with the first splitting headache she'd had in centuries.

* * *

They had been following the trail for a while, when they heard voices. A white light was visible ahead of them, probably a flashlight.

"Don't do anything. Just listen for now." Clover told her.

Madison nodded at her, watching the procession leading deeper into the forest.

She could see Jason, not so far ahead. He looked at ease

in the situation, like nothing was wrong. She could barely stop herself from rushing over to him.

"So, you have no idea what this dark mist is, huh?" Maia asked.

Jason shook his head.

"How strange. You don't remember where it came from either, do you?"

He shook his head again. Madison was confused as to why he was going along with these people. After all, he had been kidnapped by them, twice now.

Or, perhaps he was trying to get information from them. She beamed with pride. She knew she could always rely on Jason to make the best of a situation.

"What about you guys? Where do you come from? And what do you want with the Source?" he asked, sounding calm, but Madison could hear the slight shake in his voice.

Maia and Faolan gave each other a glance.

It was Lucas who replied.

"Oh well. I suppose some information is the least we could give you. We're from an organisation called the Particle Examination Commission, or the P.E.C. The primary basis is that we test the Particles present in transcenders, and try to utilise it in different forms."

He glanced behind him, at Maia and Faolan.

"One of the things we use this for is the development of artificial powers. Those fancy shapeshifting powers that Faolan has are a result of this."

Faolan only gave a grunt in response.

"And the bomb earlier on was a result of this too. It was Maia's creation, actually."

Madison shook with anger. How could Lucas talk as if nearly killing them was an achievement? Her entire body itched to move, to show them what she was capable of.

But then again, she didn't even know what she was capable of herself.

Jason turned to Maia, an unimpressed glint in his eye.

"Don't you think the bomb was a bit excessive?"

The lady shrugged, indifferent to the situation.

"We didn't want to risk getting too close to that Source guardian. And besides. It wouldn't have hurt you."

"I highly doubt that."

There was silence for a moment.

"I'm guessing the reason you want the Source is because you want to use it to base your magic research on?" Jason questioned.

The three looked at each other, insinuating that this was not the case. Lucas laughed, a harsh, forced sound coming from his lips.

"Well...it goes just a bit further than that. It's complicated."

There was a prolonged silence. Jason broke it.

"And...what do you want with me?"

Lucas looked behind him to give him a smile.

"As bait, of course! It works every time. And for another reason."

He gazed at Jason so intensely, Madison could almost feel it from where she was watching.

"There's something strange about you."

Madison paled.

She knew what they were getting to, and she didn't want to Jason to hear the news from them at all.

"We have to go to them, Clover!"

"No, we don't have to do anything. They're not harming Jason, so therefore nothing's wrong . We need to find the right time to act. And besides. I'm tired."

"But we can't just leave him there! I need to go to him."

"Were you not listening to me? I said-"

Madison stepped out from her cover, in full view of the other four. As she did so, the bright trail of blue disappeared.

"Madison!" Jason shouted, drawing the other three's attention to her.

"Ah. So you found us."

"Let go of Jason!" she snarled, a deathly edge to her tone.

In response to this, Maia reached out, gripping Jason even tighter.

"I'm sorry. But that's not going to happen."

Faolan and Lucas ran to Maia, and she took something out from her pocket while keeping a tight grip on Jason.

"No!" Madison cried.

Lucas grinned, wide and catlike as Maia raised her hand, holding something white and glowing.

Madison had initially thought it was a flashlight, but it soon became clear that it wasn't.

"I'm sorry, but this is where we depart. It was nice knowing you."

"Madison!" Jason yelled, struggling to get out of Maia's grip.

"Jason!" she screamed, running to them.

The white light expanded as she ran. They were just in her reach before they vanished in a bright flash.

Everything went silent.

Clover returned to the Source stone, looking livid.

"I told you this would happen, but of course a lowly Source guardian like me doesn't need to be listened to."

Madison just stood there, a lost expression on her face.

She always ended up like this somehow or another.

She mentally cursed herself, kicking the ground in frustration.

Perhaps she deserved what came to her.

CHAPTER 14

SHE'D LOST HIM.

And it was all her fault.

Madison wandered for ages, losing motivation steadily.

The forest she had grown to love seemed to work against her in the darkness, causing her to stumble and trip multiple times.

Jason was the only thought keeping her going.

She had to find him.

Before it was too late.

Eventually, she had to admit it. She was making no headway. She was merely walking around, hoping the direction she was going in was correct.

Then a thought came to her.

She wasn't going to find him.

Her knees buckled, and she fell sideways, knocking into

a tree. That thought alone was enough to form a lump in her throat. She felt her eyes water, but tears didn't fall.

They never did.

Madison knew the hopelessness of her situation.

So she did the one thing she could remember.

She lay down, shivering on the forest floor.

The grass prickled her cheek, icy cold.

She lay there, unsure of what else to do.

Madison stayed there for a while, the tears not quite coming out.

"Madison."

She brought her head up, looking around. She couldn't see anyone in the darkness.

The voice was soft, friendly.

Familiar.

But from where?

"Aren't you going to find Jason?"

"No" Madison found herself answering.

"Why not?" the voice asked, worry in his tone.

She sat up from her position. Something about the voice's nostalgic familiarity spurred her to continue talking to him.

"I'm lost, for one. I wouldn't be able to find him even if I wanted to. I'd have no way of fighting the other three, either."

There was a pause, and Madison wondered if the voice had left her as well.

"But don't you want to find him?" the voice asked.

"Of course I do. I'm just not able to."

"But you still can."

Madison looked up, false hope stirring in her as she

listened to the voice.

She knew better to believe him. Did he not see her situation?

"What would you know? You're probably just a figment of my imagination. I've finally gone mad, haven't I?"

The voice laughed, a tinkling sound that Madison never wanted to forget.

"I'm a bit more than that."

There was silence, and Madison, losing all hope, began to close her eyes.

"The stars are so beautiful."

This caught Madison off guard. She knew she wouldn't be able to see them through all the mist.

"Why don't you look up?" the voice asked.

"There's too much dark mist. Can't see."

"Look closely."

Having nothing else to do, she complied.

A shocking sight met her eyes.

Just past the dark swirls of mist, she could see a hint of blue. And through it, she could see.

It appeared before her in the swift breeze of the night.

The moment was like she and the earth had parted ways, leaving nothing between her and the vast expanse. The stars seemed infinite, dotting the the sky with their own pinpricks of light, apart but together in their glow. And the colours- so many consumed the sky at once, blending together to become one. Pink, violet, aqua melded together in perfect harmony. There was no dark mist, no wall blocking her from the entirety of it.

Something inside her shifted, glowing precariously.

"We all came from it", said the voice in her memory, "so we are all in the same."

She felt a strange yet familiar energy coming from all around her, from every tree, every bush and plant and flower and animal.

They were all in the same.

This was enough to remind her of where she came from.

Who she was.

And she knew exactly what she had to do. She opened the palm of her hand, calm with her newfound knowledge. Swirls of blue dust rose out from her fingertips.

That was all she needed.

The light in her hand enhanced, until she could finally see her surroundings.

She recognised a fallen log she and Jason stepped over on their way to the lake. She somewhat remembered the way back to the shore from there, and something told her that was where they were going.

Madison stood up, looking around for the source of the voice that helped her.

"Thank you, voice" she called out loudly.

She didn't get an answer.

But she knew that he'd heard her.

Undeterred, she walked ahead, with the light from her palm as a guide.

* * *

As the flash of the light died down, I found that we were

standing in a completely different part of the forest.

Lucas glanced around, and turned to Maia, a discontented look on his face.

"This isn't the shore."

Maia held up device she held in her hand, the white light dimmed considerably. "There wasn't enough energy to bring us there. We'll have to walk."

I wasn't listening to this.

"Why did you leave her there?!" I screamed, kicking and thrashing in fury, but of course, that didn't do anything.

Maia only tightened her grip on me.

"We don't need her, or the trouble she'd cause. That's just how it has to be."

"Let go of me right now!" I struggled even harder.

Madison was all alone back there, without help. She never thought she needed it, but everyone does.

She's strong, but not invincible.

"I said, let go." I growled, my desperation turning to anger.

Faolan, in his wolf form, snarled at me viciously.

"There's no need for that, Faolan. He has the right to be mad at us" Lucas berated. His head lowered.

"But he's just making more trouble-"

"Did you hear me?" Lucas's violet eyes glowed dangerously in Faolan's direction.

Faolan backed down, not looking happy in the slightest.

"Remember why you're here. Listen to what I say. Or

you won't like the consequences."

I watched, my struggling coming to an abrupt end.

It was strange, how Lucas was the youngest in the group, yet he held the authority. They listened to everything he said.

Or maybe they had to.

I didn't like this situation at all.

"What do you want from me?" I asked quietly.

Lucas looked at me, his violet eyes flashing bright for a moment. I looked away, remembering what Madison told me about his power.

"You're not normal. Yes, even by transcender standards. We just want to check something out."

I fell quiet. Were they talking about the splitting headache I had earlier? Or the hole I created?

Or the voice that sounded in my head?

"What do you mean?" I asked.

"Don't worry about it. You'll see very soon."

This only confused me more. Something told me that I wouldn't like what I was seeing in the slightest.

The forest was dark and uncertain, only heavily enforced by the unexplained cloud of mist overhead. I could barely see, and stumbled very often because of this.

The longer we travelled, the more dense the mist seemed to get.

"You are the one that made the giant hole in the middle of the clearing, right?"

I didn't answer, not wanting to give them any more information.

"Well, I guess it's only fair. We did kind of kidnap you and stuff. Here's what your friend Madison suggested to me earlier on."

He came up beside me, and I jerked back.

"We trade information. What do you say? It seemed like a pretty good deal before she decided to bail."

I thought about it for a minute. I knew how valuable information could be, and I didn't want to have to pass up an opportunity to get some. But at the same time, I wanted to avoid giving away something valuable to them.

"What kind of information?" I asked.

"Well, that's entirely up to you. As long as I know the answer, of course."

I considered for a while, until I came up with the most obvious question.

"Why do you want the Source?"

* * *

Madison had been walking for a while. In the numbing quiet, the only sound near her was the crunching of leaves under her feet.

She had been gazing at the tips of her fingers for a while, watching the blue dust spiral from her fingertips. It was comforting, for some reason. It contented her to know that she was finally with her powers.

She found her mind wandering back to the voice she had heard before. Now that she was back to her senses, it puzzled her more and more.

Was it just her imagination? Or was it something more than that? Either way, it didn't make sense, and it was annoying her that she was getting used to that.

Madison noticed that as she got closer to the shore, the thicker the mist got. She was grateful for the light coming from her hands or she would be barely able to see much at all.

As she walked, a question came up in her mind.

When she got to Jason, how would she fight the other three? She barely knew how to use her powers.

She gripped her hands tightly, and the light dimmed from her fingers.

She panicked as the glow faded quickly, and she tried waving her hands around frantically to stop it. But it didn't work.

It was gone.

Without it, it was completely dark.

All of Madison's newfound bravery quickly diminished, and her legs shook. In a desperate fit, she held her hands in front of her, trying to rekindle the light.

She didn't remember how.

Try as she might, she just couldn't recreate the glow.

"That's not going to work, and you know it" a deadpan voice came up behind her, along with a myriad of bright blue light seeping in all directions.

"Clover!" Madison cried, never having been happier to see her.

"Looks like you could use some help."

"I'd say I need a bit more than that. I don't even remember where I'm going. And I don't know for sure if they're taking Jason to the shore."

Clover stayed quiet, addressing the situation, her eyebrows furrowed in thought.

"They're going this way" she said, pointing in font of her.

"How did you figure that out?" Madison asked, intrigued. Clover looked more than a little proud of herself when she replied.

"It's just skill. Some of us are born with natural talent for things, while others just have to work their way up."

Madison sighed, regretting inflating her ego.

"Do you have a plan?" Madison asked.

Clover glared at her.

"Come on! If I do everything for you, then how am I supposed to teach you how to stand on your own two feet? Like it or not, you are the next Source vessel. You won't be at your best if I'm always doing everything for you. You come up with the plan. What are we going to do?"

This statement created a hard weight in her stomach, for some reason.

"Alright."

She sat up, surveying the area constructively.

"The Source is really the only thing we could use in our plan" she said, holding up the stone in question. It began to glow brighter as she did so.

"I have an idea" Clover pitched in.

"I thought you said you were going to let me do

things." Clover shrugged indecisively.

"Well, now that I think about it, I'd rather not. You see, you're still a kid and I don't trust you to make full decisions."

Madison took in a deep sigh, more than insulted.

"Of course. So what's your plan?"

Clover looked her straight in the eyes, and Madison caught an unfamiliar alertness in her gaze.

"It's a bit complicated, and hard to explain, so what I need you to do is trust me."

"Trust you?"

"Yes. Did I not make myself clear?"

Madison narrowed her eyes a little, but conformed to her idea, mainly because she had no other options.

It was strange. From her experience, people didn't do things for others unless they wanted something in return. Try as she might, she just couldn't think of anything that Clover might want from her.

"Alright."

"Close your eyes."

Madison complied, hoping that she wouldn't regret this.

As she did so, she vaguely saw a bright flash come out from the stone.

* * *

"Haven't we already told you the answer to that before?" Lucas asked, tilting his head to the side.

"But I want a detailed answer. What exactly do you

need the Source for?"

Lucas sighed.

"Well, if you say so. There's a... problem going on in the world at the moment."

I waited for him to continue.

"It was a problem that started with transcender magic. So we figured the only way it could be fixed was with transcender magic as well."

"So if you need the Source for it, why didn't you take Madison with us? She has it."

Lucas gave me a look, a knowing glint in his eye.

I gulped.

"After finding you, we figured we didn't need it anymore."

I paled, knowing that something was going to happen. Something bad.

Lucas' smirk only grew.

"I want you to do it."

This only served to confuse me even more than I already was.

"Do what?" I asked, my lip quivering.

"Don't play dumb. I know you know what I'm talking about. Deep down, you do."

I grew more and more agitated.

With it, the splitting headache from earlier came back at full force, causing me to writhe in pain. I gripped my head, knowing what was happening.

He was here.

He was trying to talk to me.

I'm sure you know what they're talking about.

No, I don't.

The voice sighed.

There you go again. Denying the things that you don't want to acknowledge. It gets tiring, y'know?"

"I'm not denying anything." This time, my voice didn't quite sound the same. It sounded tinny and strained.

Ugh, you're getting annoying. Let's just show them already.

"But I don't know what you're talking about!" This time I said it out loud and sure. Another burst of the headache came shortly afterwards, and I went down on my knees, clutching my head.

Don't annoy me again. Do it.

I stood to my feet, shaking from the pain. My eyes were dead and staring as I looked straight ahead.

And I complied.

The pain in my head was searing as I called on every single inch of my body to create the very essence of what I was.

Nothing.

A shocking blast of cold air rolled in from the trees ahead of me, rendering me unable to move for a minute.

Then they came.

The creatures of the dark mist emerged from the trees by the dozen. Soon so many had flown out that I couldn't keep count of them all.

I watched the torrent, my mouth agape.

Lucas gave me a wide grin.

"Thank you for complying. Now, if you would come with us?"

I backed away, cursing myself for not seeing this coming.

"No. No, that wasn't part of the deal." I stepped back twice.

"Alright, then let me put it differently. It's either we take you, or we take the girl with the Source."

I shook all over, and it wasn't from the cold.

My mind was already set. I couldn't let these guys take the Source, or there would be no way for Madison to get back. There was really only one choice.

"I'll do it."

Lucas gave me a toothy grin.

"Let's go then."

* * *

Madison opened her eyes.

She jumped back, surprised by what she saw in front of her.

It was her.

Though it wasn't exactly the same. The girl in front of her was a younger version of herself, maybe seven or eight.

Another noticeable change was that she was glowing a

bright shade of blue.

The one thing that was the same was the permanent scowl etched on her face.

"Clover, what did you do?!" she screeched, backing away instantly. Clover sighed at her antics.

"Relax, would you? Take a look around you. Do you know what this mist is? Do you know why the air is colder?"

Madison nodded, reluctantly albeit.

"Jason."

"So you did know." Clover gave her a squinting stare, trying to figure her out.

"If this is what I think it is, then we need to be very, very careful. That mist creature you saw earlier? More of those are coming."

The very mention of it made her insides shiver with fear. She always hated the reaction that ensued.

"What? But how?"

Clover gave her a strange look.

"I think you already know the answer to that."

Madison looked away, filled with new fear for Jason.

"What have they done to him? And how is this going to help us find him?" she asked, gesturing towards the strange version of her. It freaked her out a bit. All the while, she glowered at her through narrowed eyes.

Now she knew what it felt like to be on the receiving end of one of her glares.

"What you're looking at right now is a ward made of creation Particles. Those creatures are made of oblivion Particles. They're essentially opposites, so if they come close to each other, each would cancel the other out. It will protect us from them."

"But what would they do to us?"

Clover gave her a look, her gaze withholding information.

"Let's just say they would… hinder our progress. But I must warn you. Just because you're safe from them, doesn't mean that you're safe from the effects they have on your mind. All I can say is to not look at them at all. Stare at the ground like your life depends on it."

The ward hadn't taken her eyes off Madison for even a second, and it started to creep her out.

"So… why is it staring at me like that?" she asked.

"Because, it needs you to make the command. Tell it what you want it to do."

Madison gulped, stepping forward. The ward looked at her expectantly.

She cleared her throat.

"Um… lead me to Jason, and protect me from the dark mist creatures."

The ward blinked, unmoving for a second.

Then her eyes hardened, and she gestured for Madison to follow her, beginning to jog away.

"Oh, okay" Madison said, jogging after her. Clover sighed and went after them, drifting through the air.

* * *

A while had passed, and the ward's fast jog had slowed down to a walk at last. Madison stopped too, looking around expectantly.

"So, this ward… does it speak?"

"No. However, it has retained all your memories and your mindset, so communicating shouldn't be an issue between you."

Madison looked at the ward ahead of her.

"You mean... she's retained memories even from before all of this?"

"Yeah, that's what I just said."

Madison sighed defeatedly.

"And she can't talk. How helpful."

"I said that she can't talk. Not that she can't communicate."

Madison was stopped by a tight feeling in her chest.

It was horrible, a sensation which felt like her heart was being squeezed by cold slimy fingers. Suddenly she couldn't move, trapped on the spot, freezing wind seeping into her.

"Madison, ignore the feeling, keep on moving! Come on!" Clover's voice was so far away. She couldn't breathe, and it was agonizing. She heard something... somebody telling her to keep on moving. She tried it, putting one foot in front of the other. Again.

And again.

And again.

She remembered the strange voice from earlier, the stars she had glimpsed in the sky.

She remembered her goal.

As her entire being froze and her heart got numb, her resolve got stronger.

Because she would do anything for the one she loved.

Madison trudged onwards, shaking slightly from the boisterous winds and the darkness that surrounded her.

She only had one person on her mind.
That's who she was going to find.

CHAPTER 15

"MORE ARE COMING."

Madison heard Clover's voice warn her through the bright stone clenched in her fist. She steeled herself, ready to face another one of those creatures.

"I can make it. It's only one."

There was concern evident in Clover's tone.

"Actually-"

She didn't hear the rest as a freezing gale crashed into her with the weight of a winding punch.

Chilling winds swirled around her, knocking into her, stronger than they'd ever been before. She halted in her tracks, unable to move forward.

All she could see was pitch black. Darkness, stretching out in all directions.

She couldn't see.

She couldn't see anything,
She couldn't see-
Her legs buckled.
She fell.
She saw something all right.

The very sight turned her insides to jelly, her beating heart and shaky breaths the only sound to be heard for miles.

Numerous pairs of glowing green eyes stared down at her, the only thing to be seen in the darkness. She did her best not to look up.

She must not look up-
Her crouching form shook in fear-
She must not look up-
She was frozen to the bone.
She could hear voices.

They were like nothing and everything that ever mattered at the same time.

You're nothing, they said.
You are nothing.
She shut her eyes.
The beginnings of tears watered in her eyes.
But they refused to fall.
They swirled around her.
Bad thoughts.
Bad feelings.
She wanted it to stop.
Why wouldn't it stop?
Her throat was so dry.
She could barely whisper.
She could only crouch there.

Wishing and praying.

She lay there shivering, too afraid to do anything.

That's right. She was afraid.

There was a voice shouting at her. It sounded like Clover, yelling at her to get up.

To move.

It was so close.

Yet in a whole other world.

Where was the ward?

It was too late. She wouldn't be able to go after it.

Even if she wanted to.

She lifted a shaky hand to wipe the water from her eyes.

She missed them.

She missed them so much.

It seemed like an age since she'd seen Jason.

And it felt like an eternity since she'd seen the other.

Why couldn't she remember his name?

You are nothing.

You are nothing.

She forgot how long she had been crouching there.

They wouldn't leave.

"Madison."

Her heart thumped, hearing the voice's delicate tone, its familiarity giving her hope.

"Why are you lying there?"

She couldn't answer on account of the lump in her throat.

"You have to get up."

She shook her head fervently. Whatever she was going to do, it wasn't that.

"Why not?"

Through the lump in her throat, she tried to speak.

"I can't."

Silence.

It lasted so long that she believed the voice had truly left her.

"I need you to listen."

"I am listening."

"No. Not to me. To her."

So she listened.

She heard.

"Madison, get up! Listen to me! You have to let me help you if you want to get through this."

Clover's voice was all of a sudden clear.

It felt like she was hearing it for the first time.

"Did you hear her? You have to let her help you. You can't do this on your own."

She shook her head, retreating further into herself. That was one thing she absolutely refused to do.

"I can't."

"But she can help you. You have to trust her."

Trust. How could she ever trust anyone if all people did was take what they want from you and leave?

"I won't."

Clover's voice already felt more distant.

"Come on! Don't you want to find Jason? Stand up, so you can save him."

Jason.

He was the only one she could trust, right?

He was the only one who was always there for her.

Who always would be.

She needed to find him.

So she wouldn't be alone anymore.

"Jason" she whispered.

If it was to help him, maybe she could try.

The Source shone brighter, visible even through her clenched fist.

"Are you listening, Madison?" Clover's voice bellowed.

Her reply was shaky and uneven.

"I am."

"Good. Now listen to me. I need you to calm down. I'm going to do something right now, and it will help you. But it will only work if you're calm."

There was a pause that lasted a long while, Madison trying to do so.

It didn't work.

Instead, she only felt more aware of the creatures staring intently down at her.

Waiting for her to look.

"I need you to look up" the voice said.

Just the thought of doing so filled her with a compromising fear.

She squeezed her eyes even tighter, shutting out anything and everyone who could hurt her.

She found herself thinking of the promise she had made to herself when she first woke up on the island.

To stand tall, no matter what the cost.

She was filled with a slow burning anger.

She had been reduced to a cowardly crouch because of these creatures. It irritated her that she couldn't do anything to return the favour. The rage inside her grew and grew, until it became a fire.

She stood up, preparing herself to do what she had to.

She opened her eyes and looked up through her fear.

That moment was like something sparked within her, something long forgotten bubbling up inside her again.

She remembered him.

She saw his auburn hair and amber eyes.

Eyes that shone like the sun.

She remembered his name.

"Aleir."

The voice smiled.

"Good luck, Madison."

He was gone, just like that.

That wasn't the only thing she remembered. She lifted her hand excitedly. Blue dust flowed from her fingertips, glowing with a certain sureness.

Energy flowed through her body. Everything was coming back together.

But she felt anger, at the people who took Jason away.

Anger at herself, for taking so long to get to her senses.

All her energy was channelled within her, and she aimed it all around her.

It dispersed at an accelerated pace, piercing through the creatures at the speed of light.

She was so angry that she couldn't be bothered to control the extent of her power.

The vicinity filled with dust, which was quickly fading in its rich blue colour.

"You've finally unblocked your powers" Clover drifted up to her, giving her an approving look.

But Madison wasn't focusing on this.

Her eyes locked onto the glowing bright ward right in

front of her. The ward nodded at her, beginning to move again.

Madison immediately followed.

* * *

I'm disgusted with myself.

The fact that I've been the one doing this the entire time, creating the mist, the creatures, still hasn't registered completely in my mind.

What's even worse is that I hurt Madison with them.

I froze in my tracks as I remembered she was still further into the forest, no doubt looking for me.

The monsters I created went in that same direction.

I thrashed desperately, trying to get out of Maia's grip.

"What's gotten into you all of a sudden?" she said.

"Let go of me! I need to go to her!"

Lucas caught wind of the situation, walking back to us.

He gazed at me curiously.

"What's this about? You didn't seem to care much about how she was doing before. Is there something wrong?"

Just as he said that, his eyes widened, and I knew he had just figured something out.

"I know. You're only worried because the creatures you created are going after her, right? Well, it's too late for that. If you wanted to worry about her, you should have done it ages ago."

I paled, for some reason.

"You're wrong. I do care about her!"

"It sounds like you're only trying to convince yourself to me."

I don't know why this got to me so much.

Perhaps it's because he was getting somewhere.

Maybe Madison wasn't the thing I was worried about.

"You don't know much about your powers, do you?"

There was something about his tone I didn't like.

"Why would it matter to you?"

Lucas smiled at me, the gesture looking fake and superficial.

"I hope you realise that this is your chance to get some information. We're going back to a place that can give you all your answers. You can find out why you're the way you are. How you created the creatures. Or anything else you wanted to know."

I stopped.

"Why would you think I'd even consider going back with you? You've done nothing good for me."

"That's true. But there's so much we could do. If you came with us, you'd have concrete information, statistics, reliable sources of infor-"

"I hear something" Faolan spoke up from the back, looking around uneasily.

"Ignore it, it's probably just an animal. We're nearly at

the shore."

Faolan grunted none too happily, still peering around anxiously.

We trudged onwards, the pit of unease in my stomach growing heavier and heavier. I couldn't relax.

Something was wrong with Madison.

And I couldn't be there to help her.

Lucas stopped abruptly, and I soon saw why.

The hole I made stood proudly where it had been before, as big as ever.

"That's impressive. Do you think it's bottomless?" Lucas remarked.

I shivered at the thought.

"So what do you say? Will you come with us or not? And before you answer, think about what you have on the line right now."

I closed my eyes. As much as I didn't want to admit it, he was right. I wanted desperately to know what going on. What was happening to me. But Madison was another factor that I couldn't afford to leave out. I wasn't going anywhere until I knew Madison was safe.

"I-"

"Look out!" Maia yelled. In a flash, she whipped out a gun and pointed in the direction of the brightest blue light I had ever seen. I realised who it was instantly, but I wasn't fast enough to call out.

"Stop!"

It was too late. The shot had been fired.

At Madison.

Madison heard a loud scream as the bullet just barely missed her.

It was Jason.

In a blind rage she ran at the three holding him hostage.

She was out of control.

She felt unstoppable.

Faolan growled at her, changing into his wolf form. He bolted towards her, full of rage and fury.

That was fine. It merely even the odds.

Something inside her guided her, as she summoned all her power, a giant well pouring out of her core. The wolf came at her again. She dodged.

Again.

And again.

She screamed in fury, summoning all her power, but it's not enough,

not enough-

Faolan is still relentless in his attack. In the midst of their battle, she caught a glimpse of Jason.

He gave her a look full of such emotion, she couldn't bear to look away.

Relief, fear, and guilt flashed in his eyes.

This only served to make her angrier. She screamed at the top of her lungs and ran to take out Lucas-

* * *

~ 228 ~

She looked feral.

Out of control.

And it was all my fault. If only I knew what I'd been doing from the start.

 I could have protected the both of us.

What was wrong with me? I couldn't do anything of any use for either of us.

She had always been a shining star.

And I had always been a black hole, drawing things in and sucking all of their goodness.

That's what I was.

Useless.

But why didn't it bother me? Is this what other people are like? Do they feel emotion for the things that they do wrong? Lucas was right. I didn't care about Madison when she was alone in the dark forest with the monsters I created. What was my problem?

Your problem is that you just won't accept who you are. Things would automatically be a lot easier if you did, the voice sounded in my mind.

Go away! You can't control me anymore!

Control you? I've done the bare minimum. You're the one who did all the hard work.

I didn't do anything!

There you go again. Only hearing what you want to hear. Everything that I'm saying right now is the truth.

No! No it's not! The truth is what I want it to be! Not what other people make it! I'm so cold and I can't see and everything is blurry but I can see something slowly approaching and I think it's-

* * *

More mist creatures. More then Madison had ever faced before. The cold was reinforced by a hundred times. But she wouldn't be deterred by them anymore.

She was the one who was going to make them cry out in fear.

She reluctantly turned from Lucas.

They surrounded her, piling on top of her, attempting to instil their fear onto her. She wouldn't give them the chance.

She faced them all, ready, but then somebody touched her mind.

"You can't just defeat termini with brute strength or resolve." It was Clover.

"So, what do you suggest?"

"Let me lend you power."

Madison agreed to this, closing her eyes, finally trusting. She felt a brand new surge of energy flow right into her.

It was like the most intense bright spark lighting inside her. She lifted her arm to see it glowing a bright blue and sparking. She turned to the mist creatures, new strength renewing her.

"Let's do this."

* * *

Watching her was like watching the world burn.
You didn't want to look at it, but it was fascinating and
terrifying at the same time. Her entire body was alight,
exuding energy and power and life. The creatures didn't
stand a chance.

It was then that I realised.

The reason I hadn't been worried for her in the forest
was because I knew that she was strong. Stronger than me.

She could take care of herself.

Then I realised another thing.

She didn't need me, either.

* * *

Madison fought with angry tears in her eyes. She could
barely see where she was going through them.

The only reason that she fought was so she could be
with the person she cared about again. She needed him
more than anything.

And she didn't know what she would do without him.

* * *

Lucas put his hand on my shoulder as we both stared at the shining star that was Madison.

"This just re- establishes my point. She's absolutely fine on her own, isn't she? So, why do you need to go with her?"

"She came all this way for me." I muttered without confidence.

"It seems to me that she's having more fun tearing up the mist creatures you made than retrieving you."

This hit something hard in my gut.

He was right. The only thing I had done for her was cause more trouble.

I'm the one who created this whole mess in the first place.

I glanced down at the gash on the left sleeve of my hoodie.

Something must have happened in the cave as well.

But knowing Madison, she didn't want to make me worry. Why am I like this? Why was hurting people the only thing I did?

Perhaps it would be better if I left Madison.

I'm sure of it.

But suddenly there's a great bang and dust is dispersed all over the place-

* * *

Her hands moved before her mind could. She knew it wasn't her.

"Clover, what was that for?" she asked frantically.

"I need you to listen carefully to me" Clover's voice resonated in her mind.

"You're going to use the Source to create a portal. But all you have to do is to let me to take total control over your body. Just for a second. And when it's been created, I need you to take your body back, grab Jason's hand, and go in."

Madison had so many questions, but she knew that there wouldn't be nearly enough time to answer them all. But she nodded, knowing time was of the essence. She felt something shift inside of her, as if her spirit was drawing into herself, getting replaced by somebody else's.

After that, the rest was a blur.

* * *

Madison was up to something, I knew it.

And I wanted to find out what.

There was a bright flash of light coming from the middle of the dust cloud. That's where she was.

Not waiting for anything, I ran in its direction, ignoring the shouts of Lucas and Faolan. Strangely enough, they didn't do anything about me running off.

I stumbled, coughing through the dust being inhaled

through my nose and mouth and getting into my eyes.

Then I arrived.

My eyes widened and my breathing hitched.

The only thing I describe what she was making as is a portal. It couldn't have been anything else.

Her entire body was tinged with the deepest electric blue, glowing powerfully, exuding the brightest light.

She saw me and something flashed in her eyes.

She looked like herself again.

"Jason…" she said softly

* * *

When Madison came back to her senses, Jason was the first thing she saw. She smiled softly, taking in his image.

"Jason…" she said.

She extended her hand, remembering Clover's orders.

"Let's go."

* * *

"Let's go" she said.

I paled, for some reason. She looked so different, but when she smiled, she looked like her normal self again. It was almost enough to get me to smile too.

But I couldn't for some reason.

She's holding out her hand.

Why am I not taking it?

She's right there.

* * *

Why was he not taking it? He's right there.

* * *

Then I realise.
I don't want to take her hand.

* * *

The smile fell from Madison's face.
"Jason? What's wrong?" she asked worriedly.

* * *

I want to find out who I am and why I'm the way I am.
As much as I don't want to leave my best friend, it's what
I have to do.

* * *

He's crying. Why is he crying? They could finally leave.
Madison let out a little gasp. Unless-
She staggered over, about to fall.
Right into the portal.

* * *

Madison looked shocked. She must have figured it out.
 But she tripped and fell.
Right into the portal.
The next few seconds felt like an age to me. We stared at each other. Something cracked in Madison's expression.

* * *

He was leaving her.
 And she couldn't bear it.

* * *

Her hand was still outstretched. I could still grab it-

* * *

He could still grab it-

* * *

But my hand stays in one place-

* * *

And that's it. The one important person in Madison's life is gone.

* * *

The last time I glimpsed her face, she looked resigned.
Like she'd given up-

* * *

on everything. It was all pointless now-

* * *

And then she was gone.

* * *

The last view of Jason she had was quickly obscured as
she fell into a maze of colours, feeling like everything
good in her life had been ripped away.
And it had.

* * *

The portal carried Madison away, and a bright flash of
light emitted from it before it completely disappeared.
Along with Madison.
One part of me thought that I'd just made the biggest
mistake on my life. The other part of me believed that this
was for the best.
Well, the best for me.
The dust had finally begun to settle, and the mist from
the creatures was finally beginning to lift up. It's like

everything decided to go back to the way that it was with the fall in action.

I stared ahead, a blank expression on my face. What was I feeling now?

Fear?

Sadness?

Anger?

No. The answer was nothing. That's how I felt. Perhaps that was the way it should be.

"I see you've made your decision" Lucas came up to me from behind, holding on to my shoulder.

I don't look at him to confirm his assumptions.

Then I see it.

The dark consuming hole in front of me.

When I think about it, all my problems came from when I created it.

I opened my eyes. They were soulless, empty. Now that Madison was gone, presumably safe, I had nothing to worry about anymore.

Not even fear itself.

"Did you hear me? We don't have much time left, so if you don't mind? Let's go."

I turned to him, hatred overturning my features.

"That's the last thing I would do after what you've done."

Then I bounded away, sure of my location.

Faolan bolted after me, but I already had a head start.

It was too late for them.

The hole looked dark, endless and uninviting.

Like the very concept of nothing had been borne there.

That was okay.

If this is what it takes to find out who I am, then it's merely another stepping stone.

With one bounding leap, I jump into the hole.

I still don't understand why I said this.

But it seems kind of fitting for my situation.

Go back to the nothing from which you were made.

CHAPTER 16

HE DIDN'T TAKE HER HAND.

She still couldn't believe it. Couldn't understand.

Was it real? Was it a joke?

It was a joke.

It had to be.

She needed it to be.

Why didn't he take it?

He was so close.

Did she do something?

Was it her?

It was her. She realised now.

It always had been.

Perhaps it had been inevitable. Or maybe not.

If she had just trusted Clover sooner, if she had been able to get to him a little earlier.

Where was she?
It didn't matter to her.
Not anymore.
It was cold.
She was numb.
She didn't care.
Would everything be alright?
She'd won,
She'd found the Source,
She'd got off the island.
But it all meant nothing to her now.
None of it compared to what she had lost.

Maybe she'd been looking at it the wrong way her entire life.
Other people weren't her greatest enemy.
She was.

She shut her eyes.
It was so dark.
She wished she could see the stars again.

* * *

Her eyelids flickered open slowly, staring up at the ceiling. The ceiling?

She had been getting used to waking up to the sky. The ceiling was cracked and mouldy.

She blinked once, twice, before realising there was a problem.

She got up quickly, scouring the area.

She was in…a room.

The cream coloured walls were tainted with the festering of decay. The only light in the room came from a dimly lit lamp, just beside her on a desk. And...

A flower.

Its pale blue glow had dimmed considerably, weaker than it had been before.

It was the same one *he* had given her in the cave.

She turned away.

There was a mirror in the corner of the room, dusty and unused. Madison was lying in an unfamiliar bed, a thin blanket lying over her, though it still kept her warm.

Warmth.

It felt like an age since she last felt it. It enveloped her, wrapping her up in a tight snuggly hold, protecting her from the coldness of the world.

She couldn't part with the blanket, so instead she took it with her, sliding off the bed. Without really thinking about it, she walked towards the closed curtains.

As she did so, the pulse of her heart quickened, with no particular reason. She couldn't explain why she felt like this.

Her nervousness peaked as she drew back the curtain.

Her face fell.

The sky was pitch black.

No sun.

No clouds.

No stars.

Her memories had been real.

Her hand slumped back down to her side. To say she was disappointed would be an understatement.

She paced to the mirror in front of her.

Her face lacked the spark of life it once had, tinged with a sickly look. Blue eyes jumped out at her under dark bags. Her dark hair was tangled and ragged. A white shirt hung off her haggard frame, too big for her.

And not hers.

She definitely wasn't alone.

Madison took a quick glance around the room. Her old clothes weren't there, but that's not what she was worried about.

The Source had been in her hoodie.

The door stood on the opposite side of the room to the mirror, its brown mahogany gleaming proudly in the pale light. With great consideration for the noisiness, she opened it just enough for her to peak through. It was too dark for her to make out anything in particular, but she saw a yellow light coming from the space between the door across from her. She paled, knowing all too well that the person that brought her here was in there.

The door swung open.

Madison didn't know what she was supposed to do.

So she didn't do anything. Partly because she couldn't muster the strength, or any will inside her, that wanted to do so. The sleep had drained more than just her energy.

The woman who walked out of the room was barely visible due to the darkness of the hallway, but she noticed Madison's outline right away when she stepped out.

"You've finally woken up."

Madison didn't respond as the woman walked over, opening up the door fully.

"The Master told me that you were the tough one. I

expected a bit more of a reaction from you."

Her heart made a unexpected leap at the mention of the Master.

"You…know the Master?" she asked in surprise.

Madison took the chance to get a proper look at her.

She had a dark complexion and a stern gaze, which didn't look out of place on her. A grey shawl was draped around her shoulders, and crystalline brown eyes studied her curiously. She sighed.

"This probably wasn't the best introduction you've ever had to someone before."

Madison thought back to the time she threatened the Master with a pocket knife.

"I've had worse."

"Let's start over. And let's get the lights on too. It's too gloomy."

She strode over to the light switch in the corner of the room, and switched it on, giving the hallway some colour and relieving an inkling of Madison's tensions.

"First of all, I'd like to apologise for the state of this place. I haven't been here in years, and I haven't started redecorating yet. You can call me Maria. And as you could already guess, the Master sent me to get you."

Madison looked at her curiously.

"Where did you find me?"

At the ask of this question, Maria looked away, her face obscured from view.

"You were lying in the snow. You were awake, but you weren't responding to anything at all. You remember what happened, right?"

Madison closed her eyes. Those moments were blurred

in her memory, but the recollection of the numbing cold and dark hadn't left her.

Now she kind of wished she could forget again.

"Yeah, but I don't have all my memories from before this happened."

Maria sighed, shaking her head woefully.

"I don't know what that man was thinking, roping you into this mess. Well, let's talk about it. You tell me what happened over there, and I'll tell you anything that I know."

With a calming deep breath, Madison recounted the entire story of the island to Maria, who listened attentively, only interrupting with little sighs and shakes of her head.

"Obviously you've been through a lot. I don't even think talking about this right now is a good idea. Go back and rest. We can do this later."

"I want to know something first."

"Of course. What is it?" the lady asked, eyes furrowed in worry, even more so due to the recounted tale.

Madison looked up at her, a stern presence coming through in her gaze.

"What happened to the sky?"

Maria gave her a taken- aback look, not expecting that query.

"It happened a long time ago. The black mist started spreading from the north pole, and over time, engulfed half the globe. It has yet to spread to the South. Nobody knows the exact reason, only that it was the fault of transcenders." She spoke in a low voice, and Madison knew she was troubled by her own words.

Madison nodded, a hard weight setting in her stomach after learning that. Her mind shifted to another issue.

"Where's the Source?" she asked, looking around.

"The Source? Oh-" Maria gasped, realising something crucial.

"So the glowing stone in your pocket was the Source?" she asked. Madison nodded.

"I didn't expect it to look like that either."

Maria sighed. She seemed to do that a lot.

"Well, it's safe, nevertheless. I made sure of it."

She nodded half heartedly and slugged back to bed.

Her head ached, and she placed it on her pillow as she slung back into the land of dreams.

* * *

"Get up! We need to leave!"

You hear his voice through all the wind in your ears. But you choose not to listen to his words.

"No! Not without him!"

"But it's too late!"

"It's not! I'm not leaving without him-"

The wind is getting louder and the air is getting colder and your heart is getting number-

And you need to stay here, you need to find him before everything you've worked for and loved crumbles to dust-

"Madison!" Jason won't leave your side, won't stir for anything either-

Even if he was the one that caused all this in the first place-

Or whatever that thing was, the thing that-

"Madison, please! We need to leave! I know you want to

help, but-"

His voice is drowned out by a deafening sound, louder than his screams, louder than the wind in your ears, louder than anything you had ever heard-

You feel the freezing snow on your cheek, remembered how you imagined the moments where you connected with natural elements outside-

Basking in the sun-
your feet in the dirt-
snow falling into your hair-
the wind carrying your body, taking you somewhere far, far from here-
But it was different, so so different-
Your face smeared with dirt-
The snow encasing you, trapping you-
the wind knocking you to and fro-
The sun, long gone, along with your last shreds of hope-
Hope-
That's right-
you have to find him-
you have to find Aleir, before he-
The noise halts your thoughts.
It's right behind you.

Jason has gone silent.

You turn around.

A maniacal grin overtakes his features, wide and unhinged. Half his face is engulfed in a black mist, his eyes unnaturally green. The noise is deafening.

Behind him, buildings are cast in the air, the crumbling structures suspended haphazardly.

You know.

That's not Jason, anymore.

You're alone.

* * *

Madison woke up gasping, her eyes flying open. She dashed out of her bed, looking around frantically for something of familiarity, something she could have and hold and remember.

She needed to remember, remember a time when everything wasn't going horribly wrong, when she knew the world and how it worked. Dropping her thin blanket on the floor, she dashed down the stairs, looking for the glowing stone she had risked her life for.

The Source.

She ran into every single door she could find, uprooting every room.

She had to find it, find it before it all became too much for her, before everything she had worked for and loved crumbled to dust-

The light came on, and Maria walked in, looking around in shock.

"Madison, what-"

"Where is it?!" she screamed, rushing across the room. Why was she screaming? She didn't know. It was the only thing she could think of doing.

"I need you to calm down-"

"Where is it?!"

"I'll go get it for you. Just calm down" Maria spoke to her as if she were something dangerous, uncontrollable.

Was she?

She didn't even know herself anymore.

Was that why he left?

Her eyes began to water as she stared up at Maria in guilt.

That's right. That's why she was frantic.

It was him.

"I'm sorry," she said, choking back a sob, "I- I had a dream, and-"

"Don't apologise. I understand."

Madison was shocked.

Why was she being so kind to her?

Something inside her was breaking, the cracks widening the longer she stood there shaking.

She didn't have to wait this time.

The tears finally fell, feeling alien and strange on Madison's cheeks.

Maria said nothing, enveloping her in a hug on the floor.

"It's okay. Cry as much as you need to. It'll be all right."

This only caused Madison to cry harder.

How would things ever be alright if they weren't with her anymore?

She didn't know how long they had stayed like that.

It was probably a minute.

But it felt like an age.

Finally Maria let go, looking at her in concern.

"Come to the kitchen. I've held off on the 'All in One' packets for tonight. I have dinner cooking, and in the mean time you can have some nice hot chocolate."

Madison sniffed, wiping away her tears.

It was strange. Even though she was a total stranger to her, she still supported her, and when she'd just trashed her room at that.

She had been wrong this entire time.

Perhaps other people weren't her greatest enemy after all.

CHAPTER 17

THE NEXT FEW DAYS WERE EXTREMELY UNEVENTFUL.

Madison lay in bed the entire time, not wanting to move, speak or have any interactions with anybody.

Well, the interactions were inevitable.

"You still haven't gotten up yet?" Clover asked her, emerging from the glowing stone.

Madison turned her head over to the other side to block to bright light in her line of vision. That didn't do much, so she shut her eyes instead.

"You know I'm not going to tolerate this for long, right? This is a mess you got me into, and you sure as hell do *not* get to lie there while I suffer internally."

Madison stayed quiet. Partly because she knew that talking would just add fuel to the fire, and partly because she knew it annoyed her.

"And I don't even get a thank you for getting you off the island?"

Madison buried her head further into the pillow, unwilling to hear anymore.

"Ugh. Children."

"I'm not a child" she muttered from her pillow.

"Aha! So you can talk."

"Well don't get too excited, because I'm not gonna be doing it again."

"Not even for the exciting things I have to show you?"

Maria came into the room, gripping something in her hands. Not even this could get Madison out of the bed.

Clover's head snapped towards Maria.

"What is it?" she asked curiously.

Maria put the parcel down on the desk by the door.

"If you want to find out, then Madison will have to come out of bed and open it herself."

Madison pulled the cover over her tighter. No child tricks were going to work on her.

"Come on, I didn't take in a mopey teenager by accident now, did I?"

"I'm thirteen, so yes. Yes you did."

She'd remembered that fact in memory.

She got one every night, each slowly piecing back the puzzle which was her life. Some relieved the questions swirling in her mind, but most just added more. She remembered when she first woke up on the island, the freedom she had felt walking through the forest, a head empty of burdens and sorrow.

She missed that now more than ever before.

At this, Maria went to sit down at the bed beside her.

"What's this all about, now? Did you regain a bad memory?"

Madison shook her head.

Maria jolted slightly, something clicking in her mind.

"Do you...miss somebody?"

Madison was surprised by how precisely she'd hit the nail on the head.

Though she didn't answer.

"It wouldn't happen to be the boy you went on this adventure with? Jason, was it?"

Something in Madison's chest ached, hearing his name. She didn't answer again.

Maria said nothing, but leaned in closer to Madison.

"Did I forget to add that this parcel was sent to you from the Master?"

Madison leaped up faster than she ever had before, dashing across the room in one fell swoop.

She wanted to get her hands on anything she could from her past.

"Well that certainly worked" Clover commented.

The parcel was thick and rectangular shaped, but she didn't care for the exterior.

She ripped it open and shreds of paper drifted to the floor. A small rectangular piece of paper fell with the shreds.

She picked it up, examining it closely.

The handwriting seemed to spiral across the page. But something in her memory clicked, and she could read it like it was nothing.

"A note" she said quietly.

"What does it say?" Clover asked.

Madison looked over at her glowing apparition and stuck her tongue out.

Clover gasped, looking affronted.

"After all I've done for you."

Madison ignored this in favor of the letter.

Madison,

By the time you're reading this, you will have retrieved the Source. Great job! I'm super proud.

But I also know you well enough to know that you're not quite yourself at the moment.

Remember when we first met, and you'd been trying to escape? Remember I told you that a time would come where you would go to the outside world? This is only the beginning. And unfortunately, it's not as light and perfect as you thought it would be.

I also know that you're worried sick about Jason, and missing him dearly. I'd tell you not to worry about him at all, but I know that alone won't stop you! Jason's smart, and probably knows his way around things more than an adult like me! He'll come back to you, someday. He just has to deal with what he's going through alone.

I'm sure you're concerned about your memories. As you've noticed, they're returning after resting sessions where your mind recuperates. Don't worry, you're eventually going to recover all of your memories. In the meantime, you'll train with Maria. You'll grow strong enough to be able to handle to full extent of the Source's power. And after that, we'll take it as we go.

Another note-worthy thing to tell you about would be the P.E.C. I wish I could tell you that you've seen the last of them, but that isn't the case. As long as you stay with Maria, you'll be protected.

Take a look at the gift I sent you. It will give you some insight into some things concerning who you are and how you have your power.

Again, thank you for the exemplary bravery you have shown on the island. I've never been prouder of you before.

One day you will find me, and I'll explain everything properly. But for now, stay safe and work hard.

Your super awesome yet elusive mentor,
The Master

Madison looked through the letter again, checking to see that everything she had just read was real.

She couldn't believe it! She had some actual correspondence form the Master, which indicated that he was in fact still in existence.

Without wasting any more time, she grabbed the item he'd been talking about. She gasped as she saw it. She recognized it from one of her memories.

The book had no title. Its cover was plain brown, with splotches spattered randomly across it. The pages were yellow and worn.

She remembered.

This was the book that the Master and *him* were looking at in the library.

That was all she could remember of it.

She quickly put the book down.

"Is there something wrong? It's the Master, isn't it? The guy never knows when to keep his mouth shut."

Madison shook her head.

"No, it's fine."

Maria looked at her strangely.

"Are you sure?"

If she was answering honestly, no, she wasn't. There were so many questions taking up space in her mind, so many blank holes in her memory which she couldn't fill. But that wasn't what was troubling her.

There was only one question she wanted answered in that moment, one question in every moment since she'd left.

And the only person who could answer it was gone.

Madison turned to Maria, trying to distract herself.

"When do we start training?"

Maria smiled at her, while Clover let out a long winded sigh.

"About time, drama queen. If only I knew sooner that all it would take was a letter from your cru-"

"Stop that sentence right there" Madison warned.

Clover saw this as a means to annoy her further.

"Or what?" she teased. Madison went up to her, right into her bright blue face.

"Or things will get messy."

Maria looked shocked, Clover cackling uncontrollably. "Now I see what the Master was talking about."

Madison gave her a long stare, neither confirming nor denying her statement.

"Well, as you were asking, you're not going to be starting training any time soon. You need time to recuperate, to heal."

She sighed, not expecting that answer.

"Alright."

With a nod of reassurance, Maria left the room, shutting the door quietly.

Madison stared at the book she held in her hands, finding the courage to open it.

Unexpectedly, the text was handwritten, neat and tidy and small. Madison flicked through the pages, not really reading anything. She stopped abruptly at a page which had been folded over. She peered into it curiously, and a look of surprise took over her face.

An intricate painting of outer space could be viewed, one of the most detailed renditions she had ever seen. It was almost as imaginative as the projected image the Master had shown her and Jason.

She was reminded of what he had told her that day.

To look up at the stars, and be reminded that we are all in the same.

Madison stared at this picture, and her goals were suddenly clear.

She had to train her powers.

And find Jason.

Then find the stars.

* * *

The Master opened his mind, the same way he had done many times before. He felt his Particles connecting and flowing all through the world.

And suddenly, he wasn't in it anymore.

The dark expanse was vast, empty, soulless.

Like the very concept of nothing had been borne there.

Just the way he remembered.

His physical body couldn't be reached in Oblivion, so he travelled through using his Particles, filling the expanse with his presence.

He went deeper, and deeper.

The dark somehow seemed to get darker, the emptiness of the place tinging with a uneasy feeling which he could easily pinpoint.

He felt nothing, he heard nothing. He was nothing.

So he went down.

As he went even deeper, the change became more distinct. Something was lurking in the darkness, never commenting, just watching, filling his insides with a sick sensation.

He knew precisely what it was.

And what it wanted.

Unfortunately, it was the very thing he had come to take away.

Just as he thought it, he spotted it.

It shone like a tiny star in the distance, the only thing one could see for miles around.

Well, should he say, he.

The Master knew that if Jason didn't get out from this place soon, it wouldn't end well for him.

So he started on his way towards him, maneuvering effortlessly through the void of nothing and darkness.

It was amazing how Jason even managed to find his way in here. He was probably the first material being to make their way into Oblivion.

And that was why the creature of pure evil wanted him so badly.

He was finally there.

Jason was right in front of him, his tiny frame curled up as if he were sleeping.

It was funny to think how this little boy was the cause of all the devastation that happened on that day.

But the Master knew better than to judge people by their covers.

The Master surrounded Jason with his Particles, creating a gentle current to bring him in the direction he wanted.

He brought him upwards, back to the surface.

They travelled like that for a while, Jason's weight doing little to deter him.

What he found interesting was the look devoid of emotion on the boy's face.

He was curious. What exactly had prompted Jason to jump into that hole, unaware of where he would end up? Perhaps it had been curiosity, or maybe he hadn't been given any other more pleasant options. Something told him that his reason was more... complex than that. Jason was a strange kid, so his motives would be too.

Since Oblivion can only be accessed through oblivion Particles, and it didn't exist in the same way most other things did, the mind needed to imagine what it looked like.

The Master found himself wondering what Jason's nothing looked like, and if it was anything like his, empty and dark.

After a while, the strange air of suffocating darkness had been released from him, and that was when he knew that he was out of the more stifling parts of Oblivion.

The rest from here would be a piece of cake.

He created a tie. The Particles in Jason would become compelled by the high concentration of oblivion Particles in something else.

He already knew what that was.

With that, he let go of Jason, leaving him to drift to the size of a dot in the darkness. But now he had a direction to go to.

And one way or another, he would end up in the Transcender city.

The Master felt a sudden lurch in his senses.

A dark tone reverberated all around him, a chilling mix of scratchiness and a low, thudding whisper.

"I didn't realize I'd be seeing you back here so soon."

It swarmed around him, sounding like a thousand voices uttering the same words in the same tone.

The monster that resided in Oblivion.

The Master steadied his Particles.

"Neither did I. But the circumstances called it" he replied in an emotionless tone.

There was silence, but this one was stifling in its anticipation. He knew what the monster was going to say next.

"Bring the child back."

There it was.

"I'm afraid I cannot do that."

"You do not understand what this will bring upon you. This is not the first time you have dismissed my demands. You stole the Source of oblivion, and now you have come to steal what has rightfully become mine. I've been lenient with you in the past, but if you dismiss me one more time, I will not have mercy!" The monster's tone rose with every word, and its raspy voice was nearing a deafening roar by the end of its sentence.

The Master went silent, setting his sights on Jason once more.

There was no question about it. He could not leave Jason in the clutches of this monster.

He thought of Madison, the angry little girl he knew who would never leave Jason's side for anything. He wouldn't ever be able to look her in the eye again if she knew what he'd done.

And not to mention that it would simply be too dangerous to leave a transcender this powerful in its clutches.

"I will not bring him to you" the Master said, his tone absolute and final.

There was a worryingly long silence, Jason drifting further and further away.

"I have not forgotten our deal, a long time ago."

The Master felt his oblivion Particles go still.

He had not forgotten either.

It felt like a lifetime ago. He had been young and overly-confident, finding his way into Oblivion for the first time.

It had resulted in consequences he could never have begun to imagine.

The Master remembered telling Madison he didn't remember his name on the day they met. She hadn't believed him then, thought he was messing with her.

It had been the truth. The result of his foolishness.

The loss of his name. His identity.

"I have not forgotten either."

"Then you know what the consequences for your actions will be. I have waited too long for you. You have only a year left to find them."

With every word the creature spoke, the Master found his heart sinking lower and lower into his chest. Finding them in a year would be an impossible task.

Even so, he maneuvered his Particles upwards.

"Very well. I shall get them to you in a year."

The monster omitted a deep rumbling, a sound meant to resemble laughter, warbled and twisted. Although only the Master's oblivion Particles were present, it hurt his ears.

"We both know you will not find it. And when that happens, and the deal is lost, you will know the consequences for your actions when I leave."

The Master turned away, using his Particles to get to Jason. Getting him out of there was his top priority, for more reasons than one.

"That will not be a problem, for you will never leave. Not if I can help it."

"You could not fathom how far my reach extends. I have many allies within the P.E.C, and even in your precious transcender city. Nowhere is safe. My return will be inevitable."

At that, the Master decided he had heard enough, and

retracted his Particles from the expanse.

As he called back his oblivion Particles to return from whence they came, he had time to utter one last refrain.

"Go back to the nothing from which you were made."

CHAPTER 18

On the first day since the Master's correspondence, Madison read the transcender book.

She read of the origins of the Sources. She read of influential figures, of transcenders who changed the face of the earth with their power and knowledge. She read of the bitter relationship between those who could and couldn't use magic.

And she read of the emission of dark mist into the atmosphere.

The beginning of the end.

She remembered something that *he* told her on the day they had tried to escape the confinement building. That what people need is always more important than what they want.

She still found herself disagreeing.

* * *

On the second day, Madison wandered around the house.

It was bigger than she had expected, and emptier than she could ever imagine. She counted six bedrooms, four of which were unused, three bathrooms, a kitchen, and several more empty rooms. Each had a neglected aura emanating from it, unwanted, un-needed, eerily lonely and unwelcoming.

She remembered the island, the depths of the forest beckoning her in the deeper she went, the sunlight glinting off the peaceful waves of the sea. The enlightening spread of stars in the sky, exposing her to something she had never imagined possible.

Lying next to *him* as they turned their attention to a night that belonged to them.

Her body felt strangely numb.

* * *

On the third day, Maria brought her some paper and coloring pencils.

Madison knew she had only brought them as a distraction, and she appreciated her efforts. For a while she pointed her pencil on the page, unsure of what to draw. Her eye caught the dim glow of the flower on her table, which refused to stop completely. Her pencil began to scratch the page before she realized it.

She drew a cave bathed in blue, flowers blooming from

every rock, coiling around stalagmites and stalactites, hanging from the ceiling, divulging their light.

She drew a girl, similar to her, though younger, glowing a bright shade of blue, a grateful source of light amidst the darkness and uncertainty of her surroundings.

She drew a creature, shrouded in mist and darkness, indefinite features drifting in the hollows of its face.

She drew a boy, red hair drawn into a ponytail, though some still fell into his line of vision. His amber eyes sparkled with all the stars and love in the universe. His lips were drawn in the kindest of smiles.

Madison stared at the drawing.

Madison tore it in two.

* * *

On the fourth day, Madison helped Maria redecorate. She dusted and wiped and swept, reluctant to take any breaks in between. Maria had asked her several times to leave the job to her, but she ignored these requests. Any time taken to rest would inevitably bring her mind back to them.

And that was the last thing she wanted.

They soon began to paint her room, choosing a shade of light blue. Clover helped her reach higher spaces, and besides commenting one or twice about her height, didn't say much. Stopping for a vague moment, Madison watched Clover, a strange question crossing her mind. She flicked a bit of paint in her direction. It landed on Clover's luminous cloak, standing out against her sharp gleam.

So she's not intangible, Madison verified in her mind.

She tensed, the silence in the room becoming deafening, in its own way.

In a blinding flash, Clover flicked her paintbrush in her direction. She jerked as a spattering of blue stained her white shirt.

She locked eyes with Clover, accepting a silent challenge.

Madison didn't see anger, but she thought she saw a flicker of kindness and pity dash across her features. She took this a a good sign.

Needless to say, she lost the fight.

Maria wasn't too pleased to see the mess either.

* * *

On the fifth day, Madison tried to summon the ward with the Source. Clover, though greatly opposed to the idea, didn't have anything better to do.

Madison felt the somewhat familiar feeling of energy shooting down the arm which gripped the Source. When she opened her eyes again, *she* was in front of her.

Instead of the ward's aggressive stance from before, she looked resigned, even mournful. She stared, the fierce energy surrounding her contrasting her sorrowful expression.

Not knowing what else to do, Madison talked. She spoke of the island, the P.E.C, the Source, her memories, the Master. She conveyed her worries, fears and confusions about her situation. About the future.

She didn't speak about *them.*

The ward said nothing the entire time, merely staring, though Madison knew she understood.

She didn't expect what happened next. The ward opened her mouth, a pained expression turning her face, uttering the thing she refused to acknowledge by herself.

"Now.... they...they're both gone."

The words Madison was about to speak died on her lips.

With that simple sentence, a numb feeling took over her, her face crumpling.

She felt more alone than ever.

* * *

That night, she lay awake, something invisible preventing her from falling asleep. Her eyes were fixated on the window in front of her, barely visible in the darkness.

She took a deep breath, trying to register what it was that she felt.

Was it sadness?

Anger?

Hopelessness?

Somehow, the answer found its way into her mind, uninvited, unwanted.

It was nothing.

There were memories, jostling inside her, longing to be known. There were memories, lurking in the crevices of her mind, longing to be forgotten.

But there was one memory, of the night they escaped,

that she wanted to remember more than anything and forget more than anything.

Questions piled up every time she went to sleep.

But they didn't matter to her anymore.

A myriad of bright light seeped from the table behind her, and she didn't even need to look to know that it was Clover. There was total quiet. Madison spoke first without thinking.

"...I never said thank you, for bringing me off the island."

Silence.

"Or sorry. For taking the Source without knowing what it would do. Or for shouting at you in the cave. Or for not listening to you. Twice. And for not trusting you, or for taking out my anger on you and for not listening for you again when the mist creatures came and-"

She paused suddenly, realizing something. She felt something wet slip down her cheek.

"...for not being strong enough."

Madison sat there, her hands clenched on her lap, tears falling steadily.

The bright light came closer, until Clover was at her side.

She dropped something into her hand. It was the blue flower that rested on the side of the bed, untouched for weeks. It still omitted a pale light, undimmed after several weeks.

"Stand up."

Madison's gaze snapped to Clover, startled by this demand.

She wore a distinct expression which she had never

~ 269 ~

seen on her face before. Her gaze was hard, blank, only strengthened by the air of raw power surrounding her.

She stood up, the bed making an ominous creak in the darkness.

"Open the curtains."

Madison felt a leap in her stomach, taking a step forward to do so.

Her hand shook as she felt the smooth fabric of the curtain.

Her heart pounded as she drew it back.

Her breath hitched as she took in the view.

A view of darkness.

A view devoid of hope.

A reminder.

That it was all her fault.

That she was weak.

"Hold up your flower."

Madison did so.

Against the pitch black, the pale light looked even brighter, eradicating some of the darkness of the world outside.

"I never told you what your task as the Source vessel is. It is to create. This answer may sound direct, but there are many different kinds of things one can create."

Clover turned to Madison, the flicker of kindness she had seen two days ago visible again. It softened her features, her hard expression melting into a warm smile.

"One of these things is hope. You may not realize this, but you are a person driven by hope. It guides you through the toughest times. You draw strength from it, and so much more."

She turned her face to the window, her glow brightening the glass.

"The Source of creation has been absent from this world for far too long. Now there is less hope in this world than ever before. And it will only get worse if we don't do something. If your job is to create, then you must create new hope. Like that flower, you'll create a bright glow to extinguish the dark."

Madison took time to process that, wiping away her tears with a little snuffle.

There was quiet, as she kept her eyes on the glowing flower, brighter than she had ever seen it.

She remembered the person that gave it to her.

And the person who'd shown her what was beyond the dark.

"I have also said things that I regret. I'm sorry for our argument in the cave, and for leaving you alone in the forest."

"I'm sorry too" Madison whispered.

"You have nothing to be sorry for. You were scared and confused."

Madison looked at Clover, a newfound light in her eyes.

"So you *are* able to be nice."

At that, Clover reverted to her natural form, a scowl forming on her lips.

"And that's probably the last time I'll ever be it. To you, at least. Now get to bed, before you give me another headache."

Madison complied, a warm feeling glowing in her chest. She crawled under the covers, not before closing the curtains, and setting her flower back on the table.

She'd already begun to feel her eyes droop, but before she went to sleep, she had time to say one last thing.

"Clover?"

"Yeah?"

"Thank you."

"For what?"

"For being here."

* * *

On the sixth day, she did what she was dreading to do from the beginning.

On the sixth day, Madison went outside.

She didn't know what had prompted her to do so, for even a peak outside her window knotted her stomach in grief and regret. But the faithful voice that spoke in her mind told her that she would have to, some day.

And here she was.

The cold bit into her first, chilling winds zipping to and fro, ensnaring her in its icy grip.

Her eyes could see, but just barely. A streetlamp on the side spattered weak light on her surroundings.

Empty,

Lifeless,

Alone.

That's right. Nothing's changed. She's alone. She's-

She looked up at the sky. Her breath hitched in her throat, gazing up at the black depths.

But she saw more than that.

It was more than that.

Even the dark told a story.

Her story, a life of struggle and confusion, of love and loss.

It was the story of countless victims of grief and struggle and pain.

But... it was also a story of hope.

Madison remembered hearing the voice, Aleir, back in the forest, when she was lost, treading around in a hopeless stumble.

He told her to look up.

And through the darkness, she saw the light of all the stars of the universe.

She had seen it.

It was there.

Just past the dark.

She thought of Jason, who had been at her side since the beginning. Of Aleir, who never didn't have a kind word for anyone. Of the Master, who could be anywhere at this given moment.

Just because they weren't with her didn't mean they were gone. She could still find them. Like the stars.

She took the glowing flower out of her pocket. It looked as bright as it had on the day Jason had given it to her against the black of her surroundings.

At her touch, it fell apart, individual petals dispersing, crumpling to dust. The wind carried it on its journey, sweeping it high above Madison's head, into the world beyond. As she watched it, she allowed herself to smile for the first time in ages.

She'd find them.

It was only a matter of time.

* * *

How long has it been?

Since I've seen something other than darkness.

Since I did something.

Since I felt something.

Is this what nothing is?

There isn't black, darkness like I thought.

There's...red.

Red crystals, glowing earnestly in this everlasting void.

It's cold.

But I'm starting to get used to it.

He *never liked the cold.*

He was always so kind, so warm, yet...

I can't remember anything else about him.

I remember, but only in bits.

She offered me her hand.

I didn't take it.

Why didn't I?

I... I think I was scared.

Of everything.

Being nothing is easier than being something. Perhaps I've already found who I am.

But something tells me I haven't.

I'm going somewhere. My whole body is moving.

But I don't know where.

I'll just leave it be. Perhaps I should do that for once.

I feel...I feel like something's coming.

Coming slowly, yes, but coming nevertheless.

And I know.

It's only a matter of time.

ABOUT THE AUTHOR

Ifunanya C. Ogochukwu Ndinojuo was born in Dublin, Ireland, with parents from Nigeria. She writes fantasy stories with a diverse set of characters, mystery, and tons of excitement. When she isn't writing, she's watching anime, playing piano or reading books.

Made in the USA
Monee, IL
10 August 2023

40662226R00164